PRAISE FOR
THINGS WE SET ON FIRE

"Reed is fearless in nudging her characters toward disaster, and the reader follows with a thumping heart, confident in the story's authoritative prose and, ultimately, redeeming spirit. I was genuinely moved by this novel, and recommend it highly."
—Antonya Nelson, author of
Bound: A Novel and *Some Fun: Stories and a Novella*

"With striking lyricism, sly humor, and great sympathy for her finely drawn characters, Deborah Reed has written a beautiful novel about family and forgiveness in *Things We Set on Fire*. I couldn't put it down, which is the kind of problem that I think every book lover hopes for."
—Christine Sneed, author of *Little Known Facts* and
Portraits of a Few of the People I've Made Cry

"Deborah Reed is one of my favorite new writers, and *Things We Set on Fire* would be an excellent introduction to her work, if you are still among the uninitiated. Here we have three generations of women, separated by space and circumstance, unexpectedly pulled back into each other's lives as though sucked into a vortex. And this is where Reed takes us: the eye of the family storm. From the intense opening scene of this kaleidoscopic, largehearted novel to its last page, there's not a dull moment here, folks."
—John McNally, author of *After the Workshop*

THINGS
WE SET
ON FIRE

THINGS
WE SET
ON FIRE

DEBORAH
REED

lake union publishing

Reed

Printed in the United States of America.

Published by Lake Union Publishing, Seattle

www.apub.com

ISBN-13: 9781477809518
ISBN-10: 1477809511
Library of Congress Control Number: 2013941698

For Jack Driscoll

AND SLOWLY I WOULD RISE AND DRESS,
FEARING THE CHRONIC ANGERS
OF THAT HOUSE.

—ROBERT HAYDEN

PRELUDE

THIRTY YEARS AGO VIVVIE REPLACED the frayed laces in Jackson's work boots with bright red ones, telling him they were all Roth's Grocery carried in that length, telling him the clash of tan boots and red laces provided him a certain style, like a woodsman. A Florida woodsman.

The following day Jackson went into the woods behind their house on Turtle Dove Lane, and Vivvie went, too—not that he could see her crouched along a squeezed corner of the Crooked River. His shoelaces were eye-catching, dizzying through her rifle-scope from fifty yards away.

A trace of juniper, like gin, surrounded Vivvie's head. She'd tethered Big Boy to her ankle once he brought her to Jackson, but her husband's scent, so close, caused the hound to tug, and Vivvie forced him down, knowing she was asking too much. Big Boy loved Jackson, everybody loved Jackson. No one more than Vivvie.

She watched as her husband dug through his vest pocket and pulled out a turkey call. He was poaching, the season still two weeks away, and he hadn't worn his orange vest, hadn't told anyone but Vivvie he was coming, and this was how she came to the idea. Her eyes stung when he'd practiced the piercing call on the porch, and again here as his trills warbled through the trees.

Vivvie's small hands were nearly palsied the way they trembled. She lowered the rifle to search for a breath, to fight the urge to run and fall into Jackson's arms and hide from the very thing she had planned against him. Elin and Kate were too young to be left home alone, and yet Vivvie would not be rushed. She set the rifle down, massaged the dog's neck, and drove the hair from her face long after the strays had settled behind her ears.

Rifles cracked off shots in the distance. Deer hunters—any one of whom could have mistaken Jackson's camouflaged coloring for a buck.

Vivvie raised the barrel, pressed the cold scope to her eye just as Jackson spit out the call, held his fist to his mouth, and clenched his eyes as if seized by pain or prayer. At her feet, a soft wavering moan grew into a searing bellow.

Big Boy lunged and Vivvie was airborne, dragged across brushwood that hiked up her jacket and tore the skin from her backbone. A line of breathy curses meant nothing to the dog. When the leash finally snapped free Big Boy kept running, and Vivvie scrambled like a soldier on the ground, latched onto the rifle, and now Jackson's throat was magnified, flecks of whiskers encompassed in a halo so close she could have been lying next to him, kissing the long tendon from collarbone to jaw. And there was Big Boy licking syrup off Jackson's jeans from the plate that'd slipped his hands at breakfast. Jackson was laughing. She thought he was. Laughing, and looking for her.

The blast echoed a white, high-pitched silence in Vivvie's ears.

She lowered the rifle and turned toward home, toward Elin and Kate, just the three of them now, a mother and two children from here on out, and Vivvie did not look behind her, only above in search of what Jackson had last seen. The sun, blazing through holes in the moss, a ceiling of tattered, filthy lace.

PART ONE

ONE

THE CALL CAME IN THE middle of the night, and at first Vivvie stood in the dark near her bed, trying to make sense of the hour. She fingered the grooves of wainscoting in the hall and into the kitchen, saying "Who on earth?" midway to lifting the receiver.

Wink's floodlight next door cast off her appliances, shooting silver sparks of light in Vivvie's eyes. She drew the curtain above the sink to see their joined yards glowing like a football field in the rain.

"I'm trying to reach Vivien Fenton?" a young man was saying, but rain crashed the tin roof like pellets, making it difficult to hear.

"For heaven's sake," Vivvie said.

"I'm with the Orlando police."

She let go of the curtain and plugged her ear. "This is Vivvie," she said, and walked into the hall where it was quieter.

"Mrs. Vivien Fenton?"

"Yes?"

He apologized for the time, said his name was Tyler Moore. Officer Tyler Moore. And then, "I need to ask if you have a daughter named Katherine. Her father's name is, well, *was* Jackson Fenton?"

Vivvie switched the phone to her other ear as if what the man was saying might be better understood over there. "Kate's my daughter," she said. "Why?"

"There's been an accident, ma'am."

"What kind of accident?"

"I believe your daughter took too many pills—I'm afraid you'll have to check with the hospital."

"You mean an overdose?"

"They can tell you everything."

"But she's all right?"

"I can give you their number."

"Are you sure it's the same Katherine? I haven't seen my daughter in years. She's not even in the state."

"Well, ma'am. She is now. Down at Orlando Regional. And your granddaughters are here with me."

"Oh," Vivvie said, or thought she had, as Officer Moore explained what an impressive eight-year-old Averlee was, calling 911, looking after her little sister until help arrived. But the girls were shaken, he said, and the younger one—what was her name again?

"Quincy," a small voice insisted in the background.

"Quincy," the officer said, "doesn't feel so well."

Vivvie covered her eyes. She never dreamed this was how it would happen—Kate and the girls returning by way of a midnight call from the police.

"She seems to be running a temperature."

Was he talking about Kate now, or Quincy?

"What I'm getting at is we need some family who can assume temporary custody of these girls."

"*Custody?*"

"Yes, ma'am. There doesn't appear to be a father in the picture."

Vivvie walked the hall.

"Social Services tells us they can't place the girls together, not tonight anyway, but if you're—"

"Where are you? What part of town?"

"Binion Road, where it intersects Orange."

"How'd you get my number?"

"Records at the DMV."

Vivvie peered into her bedroom for something, she didn't know what, something, she guessed, for wearing in the company of doctors and police. Her white oxford shirt and black pants from Roth's Grocery lay over the busted kitchen chair in the corner.

"Ma'am?"

The rain suddenly quit, and for a moment there was nothing but a quick, steady calm. The spare room—a mess of boxes, dust, and clothes she no longer fit—hadn't been used in years. And she had bleach under the kitchen sink, but of course the girls were no longer toddlers from six years ago, sleeping in a playpen, trying to get at the poisons.

"Ma'am?"

"All right," she said, her stomach hot and sick. "It's going to take me some minutes. Have they got their things with them?" It crossed her mind to go next door and ask Wink for help, his floodlight finding her again through the crack in her drapes. But no. She wouldn't do that. Wide awake now, she couldn't think of a single person to call.

Half an hour later Vivvie traveled the two-lane truck route north of the theme parks where an eagle had nested atop a telephone pole. Eagles lived long lives and Vivvie wondered if the same bird she'd brought Kate and Elin to see, with a cheap set of binoculars, still lived up there, decades later. They never did see it, the girls too busy fighting over the binoculars. She should have purchased two sets, which she realized the instant they pulled off the road, but for once in their lives they might have shared, might have shown the slightest bit of cooperation. They weren't out of the pickup more than five minutes when Vivvie got tired of pointing, tired of saying cut that out or else, tired of saying for God's sake she's your sister, and ushered them back into the cab without witnessing so much as a feather.

The police station's parking lot was nearly deserted when Vivvie shut the engine down, opened the window, and sat until the smell of acidic soil and wet pine stuck to her skin. Five in the morning, and the running lights around a billboard claiming "You'll Never Die of Thirst at Gilligan's Hideaway in Orlando" flickered into the nearby trees. The last time Vivvie was in a police station was 1974, when the cops smoked cigarettes with her and apologized for asking so many questions. They offered her coffee cake. "We may never have an answer," they said. "No other hunter has come forward to claim that the bullet might have been his." They were sorry for her loss. It was tragic, they said. *Senseless.*

Vivvie wrenched herself from the truck and into the billboard lights flashing like cameras reflecting in small puddles and in the nylon sheen of her windbreaker. Across the lot the station's windows and glass door were warmly lit, like a holiday house full of people waiting for her to arrive.

She stepped inside, and a voice opposite the lobby said, "You must be Mrs. Fenton." Two young girls with wild blond curls stood on either side of the officer who must have spoken, must have been the one who'd called her on the phone, but right now all that registered was Quincy, a flimsy-looking six-year-old, wiping her nose on the back of her hand. She had just learned to crawl when Vivvie last saw her, white dumpling hands plopping on the floor before her. And Averlee, now grown into a stony-faced eight-year-old, but her eyes still clear and blue as Fanning Springs.

Vivvie's throat squeezed so hard she had to cough to shake it loose.

The officer stepped forward and shook Vivvie's hand. The deep color of his skin blanched the girls' even more, and Vivvie wondered if they never got out in the sun.

"We have a few papers for you to sign," Officer Moore said. He stepped back and Vivvie did the same, stuffing her hands deep inside her pockets.

She studied the girls for a clue of where they'd been, what they'd witnessed, whom they might have been living with. Neatly dressed in white T-shirts and khaki shorts, white anklets rimming the tips of clean sneakers—one red pair, one blue. No shark-tooth necklaces from the beach, no hippie fashions from a commune, no cowboy boots from out west—nothing to give their lives away.

She didn't know what to say. "Averlee, you look so much like Elin," she said, which was true.

The girl didn't move.

"Do you know who Elin is?"

Nothing. Vivvie wasn't sure she'd heard.

"Elin. She's your aunt. Your mother's sister."

Averlee stared up at the officer.

Moisture clung to Vivvie's face and chest. "Well," she said, pointing to the Publix grocery bag at Averlee's feet. "Those your things?"

"Averlee threw some stuff together," the officer said, and handed Vivvie the bag. "She did a pretty good job."

Vivvie peeked in at shorts and T-shirts, a coloring book, and loose, chewed-up crayons. "Your toothbrushes in there?"

Averlee nodded.

"All right." Vivvie handed the bag to Averlee. "Let's get to signing those papers then." She stepped to the counter, lifted a blue pen with "Josephine's Auto Supply" written on the side, and clicked the spring in and out, the only sound in the room.

"You say their mother's over at Orlando Regional?" she whispered.

"That's right." The officer placed several papers on the counter in front of her. "We'll need to see some ID."

"Quit wiping your nose like that," Averlee said.

Quincy faced the door and wiped it again.

Time was playing tricks on Vivvie. She had to tell herself that these girls in need were not hers, that she was not their mother. They belonged to her daughter, a grown woman laid up in the hospital by her own hand.

Vivvie glanced at the officer and then the papers. "Too much of a prescription?" she asked.

"That's what they said."

Vivvie climbed behind the steering wheel while the girls peered through the open passenger-side door as if into a cave. Averlee set her bag on the floorboard, stepped up, and dug the middle seat belt out from between the seats. Decades of dirt and gum wrappers slid free of the seam, and Averlee and Vivvie brushed everything to the floor. Then Averlee hopped back out. "Go on," she said, nudging her sister like a little mother. Quincy got in quickly, as if on a dare, and pressed her tiny bones against Vivvie. Averlee clicked the middle belt across Quincy's waist, pulled the door shut with a grunt, and closed the three of them in.

The old Ford 150, a sturdy truck for thirty years, had belonged to Jackson, and that was all that mattered until Vivvie saw it through her granddaughters' eyes: dirty black and rusted edges, a slick vinyl seat leached with cigarette smoke, springs bursting past the brittle orange foam. Paper coffee cups littered the metal floorboard, and they, more than anything, embarrassed her. How hard would it have been to throw them away? The engine took its time catching, and when it did, the muffler bellowed like a Harley.

"You girls like grapefruit?" Vivvie asked as she popped the gear into place and circled back onto the road.

Neither said a word.

"I don't have any kind of breakfast cereal at home. Does your mother feed you grapefruit?"

"No," Averlee said.

"No what? You don't like it or she doesn't feed it to you?"

"She doesn't feed it to us so I don't know if we like it or we don't," Averlee snapped.

"Well, now." Vivvie kept her eyes straight ahead. "You use that tone with your mother?"

Averlee leaned her head against the side window.

Vivvie thought to mention the eagle nest on the telephone pole but didn't feel like talking, and anyway it was too dark to see. She pulled a cigarette pack from her purse, thought better of it with the girls, and stuffed it back in.

"What about peanut butter?" Vivvie asked.

"She feeds it to us and we like it," Averlee said.

"Is that right."

Minutes later the sky began to fade from black to midnight blue and a cattle field cut through the pines, revealing a pink horizon. Turkey vultures circled above the sunrise. "Look there," Vivvie said, surprising herself with the friendly outburst, but the sight was wondrous—as if she and the girls were on their way to catch a flight, or take a road trip to the mountains, some place fun so early in the morning. "The early bird gets the worm," Vivvie said.

"My sister has a fever," Averlee said, her eyes locked on Vivvie's. "And her throat hurts, too."

Averlee's resemblance to Elin was so striking that Vivvie could only bear it seconds at a time. She asked Quincy how she was feeling.

"Not good," Averlee answered for her.

"Uh-huh," Vivvie said. "So bad she can't talk?"

In the silence Vivvie patted Quincy's warm knee. "I understand you're feeling sick."

Quincy nodded with what looked like a loosely fitted head.

"We'll stop at the drugstore and pick something up. How long have you been sick?" Quincy didn't answer. "How long has she been sick, Averlee?"

"A few days."

"Did your mother know this?"

Averlee shrugged toward the dawn racing through a grove.

Vivvie stopped at a blinking red light and felt a new rush of the sour, yellow sickness she'd been fighting since answering the phone. She swept her hand inside the bottom of her purse, then realized she'd left her last packet of antacid on the kitchen windowsill at home.

The girls watched as she dropped the purse beneath her knees.

A car honked from behind. Vivvie checked the girls as she moved through the intersection, two sets of owl eyes peering beneath white curls. Averlee brushed the hair from her sister's damp face, held her palm against Quincy's forehead, dropped it, and let go a small, tired sigh.

Vivvie drove on, nearly reaching the drugstore before Averlee spoke again. "We only like it with grape jelly," she said. "And soft bread. Not the kind with crust. Quincy's losing her baby teeth."

It took a moment for Vivvie to realize Averlee was referring to the peanut butter.

"You see these?" Vivvie tapped a front tooth with her fingernail. "They're fake. I don't go for that tough crust myself."

TWO

VIVVIE UNEXPECTEDLY VEERED SOUTH TOWARD the hospital, unable to tolerate not knowing, not seeing what kind of shape her daughter was in. Six years since Vivvie laid eyes on her, six years since getting any kind of word that she was even alive, and now every moment she'd endured had collected inside her at once.

She set her granddaughters in front of cartoons in the nearby waiting room, handed each a juice box, and told them not to move.

"Why can't we come?" Averlee asked.

Vivvie pulled two mints from her purse. "Here. You'll see her soon enough," she said, and asked the nurse across the hall to keep an eye on them.

After that she stood clutching her purse near the door inside Kate's room, unable to approach her daughter's bed. Kate's doll-like body was propped to a near sitting position, skeletal arms at her sides, her face rawboned and pastier than Vivvie had ever seen on a living person. Tubes streamed from her nose, mouth, and arms, others snaked from beneath the sheet, impossible to tell where each began, what was their intention, whether they were feeding something toward the beeping apparatus and clear liquid bags or funneling the life back into Kate.

A thin-haired doctor fussed with an IV on the opposite side of the bed. He was slower than Vivvie when he moved but nearly half her age.

"Good God." Vivvie's voice lingered, small and stupid, in the air above her head. She needed to make sense of what was happening even as she fought off the dawning that no such sense would be made. Kate's hand twitched as if zapped by an electrical shock. "It's not a coma, right?" Vivvie said. "The nurse out front said it wasn't a coma."

"No, ma'am," the doctor said. "Just a slumber." He didn't meet her eyes.

The door behind her swung open, and a paunchy, red-haired nurse burst past Vivvie, her scrubs covered in miniature bears as if she'd just been retrieved from the pediatric ward. She tampered with a square, blue device near the bed, repositioned the wispy tubes in Kate's nose, sighed, and looked around as if for another task.

Kate was a child again—arms, legs, feet small as a schoolgirl's.

"Are you Mom?" the nurse asked, but didn't glance in Vivvie's direction, didn't look up from the clipboard now in her hand.

Vivvie nodded. "Yes."

Kate inched her head in Vivvie's direction.

"Shh, shh, shh," the nurse said, patting Kate's shoulder. Kate's lids peeled open to reveal what looked like a set of bloodshot tumors.

Vivvie backed against the wall. A moment later Kate's eyes closed, the corner of her mouth upturned as if she were dreaming something sweet.

"They do that sometimes," the nurse said. "She's not conscious. Not yet."

"How long is she going to be like this?" Vivvie asked, hearing the grope in her voice.

Kate coughed, deep and guttural.

"She's not breathing on her own?" Vivvie asked.

The nurse fastened the tube in Kate's throat. Kate's eyes shot open, closed.

Vivvie stepped forward, then back, dropped her purse to the floor, held one hand to her stomach, the other to her throat while the nurse stroked the hair from Kate's forehead.

"You just relax, Miss Katherine," she said. "Lie still."

But Kate appeared agitated, her throat jerking upward, a gurgling repetition of something that sounded an awful lot like "Get her out."

"They say things." The nurse patted Kate's arm, making it appear even smaller. "Nonsense."

The heat in Vivvie's face made her dizzy.

The doctor shot clear fluid into Kate's IV. "There's no reason she won't make a full recovery. From the pills, I mean." Vivvie didn't care for his tone. He still hadn't met her eyes, and a feeling came over her that these two were somehow blaming *Vivvie* for the pills. Blaming her for some awful childhood years.

"This isn't my fault," she said.

The doctor slid his hands into his flat white-coat pockets and peered above the rim of his glasses on his ruddy red nose. From the front he was older than his scrawny shoulders first led her to believe. "Of course not. The social worker has some information for you. She'd like to speak with you about the next steps."

Vivvie acknowledged his words with a squint.

"It's always good when the whole family participates in the recommended treatment," he said.

"I *am* the whole family," she said, and the crack in her voice made her madder than she already was.

For the first time since walking in she had their full attention.

"That's fine," the nurse said.

"Is it?" Vivvie snatched her purse from the floor.

"The recommended treatment and remedies—" the nurse began.

"*Remedies?* Look at her. You talk like all she needs is orange juice and exercise."

"It's not that," the doctor said.

Vivvie waited for an explanation.

"Due to patient privacy laws we aren't supposed to tell you," the nurse said. "All I can say is she's been in before."

Vivvie walked out, an ancient anger burning all the way to her ears. So many years of worry, her daughter's entire life a cause for worry, all a lead-up to this. Vivvie clamped her jaw to keep from swearing.

Her granddaughters had slumped sideways, one into the other, on the verge of sleep in front of the television.

"Come on, girls." Vivvie clapped her hands and turned to leave. Averlee and Quincy wriggled, half-lidded, off the chairs. She never should have come straight here. They were exhausted. She was exhausted.

"Did you see Mommy?" Averlee asked.

"Oh, I saw her all right."

"Is she okay?"

Vivvie held the doorframe, trembling so hard that passing out seemed a good possibility.

Quincy wiped her nose on the back of her hand.

"There's nothing wrong with your mommy that a swift kick in the ass won't fix," Vivvie said, kneeling in front of Quincy, digging her nails into the carpet for solid ground. "I didn't mean that. Never mind what I said. . . . How about you stop wiping your nose on your hand?" Vivvie found a tissue in her purse and swiped the snot above Quincy's lip. "Next time I want you to ask for a Kleenex."

Quincy's eyes were the same smoky grey as her father's, and Vivvie made a point not to hold it against her. "You haven't said a word since I picked you up this morning," Vivvie said. "Are you feeling any better?"

A quick, single nod swung her curls forward.

"Say, 'Yes. I feel better.'"

"Uh-huh," Quincy said.

Vivvie stuffed the tissue in Quincy's pocket and caught a glimpse of Averlee's face in the hospital light. White crust wedged in the corners of her hollowed eyes, sleep-deprived, Vivvie guessed, nights stretching beyond this one here.

"What exactly happened, Averlee? I mean at home. With your mother."

Averlee shrugged.

"How'd you find her? What was she doing?"

"I don't know. Sitting at the table with her head down."

"Why were you up so late?"

Averlee reached for her sister's hand. "Getting something for Quincy's throat."

Vivvie paused. "Did your mother say anything strange before you went to bed?"

Averlee shook her head.

"How's she been feeling lately? These last few months?"

"Okay."

"Nothing out of the ordinary going on?"

"I guess not."

"All right," Vivvie said. "That's fine. You don't have to tell me now."

Vivvie stood quickly, feeling her weight in her knees. She shook her legs out and then dug inside her purse for her cell phone. "Let's go," she said, already walking, glancing back to see they were following, a wispy mix of skinny legs and puffy, tired eyes, reams of wild hair like some physical reaction to all the chaos.

"Stand by the exit door over there," Vivvie said at the entrance. "I need to make a call."

The girls pressed their faces into the glass, hands cupping eyes like binoculars.

Before Vivvie finished dialing she realized it was the middle of the night on the West Coast. She shut the phone off and coughed into the crook of her arm, old cigarettes and stomach acid on her tongue. She popped a mint into her mouth.

The girls rolled their backs to the glass and peered up at her.

"I'm sorry about that," Vivvie said, gesturing toward the waiting room. "What I said. I was just upset. Your mother's going to be fine. . . . It upset me. That's all."

They eyed one another like puppets relaying messages in a play—*Get us out of here. Away from this old witch.*

Cool air played across the back of Vivvie's neck. She could only imagine the things Kate had told them about her, and in her imagining she was filled with the urge to tell them about their *own* mother, starting with the time Kate took a pair of scissors to half the house while Vivvie hung a basket of wash outside on the line. When Vivvie came inside she stopped in the living-room doorway, confused by the sun shining through the lower half of the windows where the drapes used to hang. Her copies of *Ladies' Home Journal* were glossy, sun-reflective flakes on the floor, her lopped-off shirtsleeves laid out on the coffee table between the laces of her shoes.

Vivvie shielded her eyes from the hospital lights. "Mercy me," she said, her mother's words from the past clamoring up inside her. All kinds of particulars needed tending to, and this put her in mind of her mother—*mercy me*, she'd say before clearing the dishes, *mercy me*, pulling weeds. *Mercy me*, Vivvie's shifts at Roth's would have to be covered. Groceries, *mercy me*, the right kind, things she never bought. . . .

And then what?

"I've got a porch swing," Vivvie said, picturing the girls happy at her house, wishing the laughter and swinging into being, eating cookies with lemonade on the screened-in porch. She needed cookies and lemonade.

Averlee stared at her.

"It stands up," Vivvie said, looping her arms into the shape of the swing. "With a frame. Not the kind that hangs from the ceiling."

Averlee's expression was unchanged.

"A porch swing. For swinging on," Vivvie said.

"What else would it be for?" Averlee said.

Vivvie reached for a cigarette, her eyes never straying from Averlee's. She stuck the cigarette between her lips, then pulled it back out.

"If you aren't the spitting image of Elin," she said, wiping the nervous grin off her own mouth. Come back to haunt me, she thought. Come back to punish me, once and for all.

THREE

WISTERIA OBSCURED THE GUTTER OUTSIDE Elin's bedroom window. She swung open the pane and stuck her head out as if from a porthole. It hadn't rained. Nothing but morning birds and sunshine—the white tip of Mount Hood visible from sixty miles away. So where had the noisy drip come from? The bathroom faucet again? Elin slammed the window so hard a screw popped free of the hinge.

"Screw you, screw," she said.

Fluke stretched in his fleece bed at her feet. "Not yet," Elin said, and his body tensed, waiting for her hand signal, a salute, to tell him it was time to rise. She didn't know if all Jack Russells were this obedient, but Fluke was committed to doing things by the book.

With Rudi already in the shower, Elin couldn't listen for the faucet. When had he gotten out of bed? She was tired, having slept little after the call from Kate at two in the morning Florida time, eleven o'clock hers. It was the first she'd heard from her sister in six years, and Kate hadn't made much sense, her snippets of conversation strange, like someone tasked with describing family photos, her words slow and slurred, submerged in a kind of drunken nostalgia. This was new. Elin had never known Kate to drink. She'd especially never known her to wane toward sentimentality. But here was her sister, the disappearing hard-luck waitress, the brooding poet who scribbled four-letter poems in notebooks in the middle of the night, who'd thrown fists and shoes at Elin's head, now harping on the phone, "And the ssssand castle I made that day. And our yellow and rrred bikinis. The waaaves . . ." Even stone-sober Kate wasn't known for making good sense, and this was reason enough for Elin to let it go. They'd never been close. Far from it. But Elin *couldn't* let it go. Her sister's voice had wormed past the sheath of Elin's nerves, especially when Kate started in on the time she'd nearly drowned. Elin had been the one to save her. So why this? Why now? Perhaps getting closer to midlife was hitting Kate hard, causing a panicked knee-jerk making of amends.

Not long after falling asleep Elin became trapped inside the same nightmare she'd fought off as a kid—the ocean, Kate's deathly pale face, the nauseating smell of Coppertone. When Elin finally managed to reach another slumber in the early morning hour, the nightmare returned, and she woke kicking the blanket to free her legs of Kate's hair, like seaweed, in the dream-ocean from which Elin gasped for breath. After that she lay awake listening to the drip, or maybe the thumping of her heart, or maybe the vein in her temple. At some point Rudi had slipped out of bed without her noticing.

Fluke sat at attention, straining for the salute so he could tear down the hallway, claws slipping and ticking the wooden stairs for his bowl in the kitchen. The anticipation built in his cocked little head, his front paws kneading the fleece. She loved this dog, his soft, small body often toted in her arms, all bright white fur except for the two perfectly brown bull's-eye markings circling each eye. She didn't know what to make of herself, taking pleasure in holding him back.

Steam from the shower drifted around the bathroom door across the room, and Rudi began whistling one of the many folksy German songs Elin would never learn. She saluted, said, "Breakfast," and then cringed as Fluke knocked his hip into the doorframe on his way out of the room.

"Good morning," Elin shouted through the bathroom door.

"What?" Rudi said.

She stuck her nose in the warm, swamp-like steam, thought again of Florida, of Kate, and steadied herself against the trim. She needed to call her mother, fill her in about Kate, even though Elin still had no idea where Kate was—no matter how hard she'd pressed, Kate refused to answer, and the number she'd called from was blocked.

The first hint of a headache flared behind one eye. Elin considered going back to bed. "Nothing," she said.

"What?" Rudi asked.

"I'm up," she said. "Going to start the water for coffee. Are you having some?"

"No, thanks. I've got to run."

Downstairs, Elin shuffled into the kitchen, put the kettle on, scooped the coffee into the French press, and fetched *The Oregonian* from the porch.

Fluke paced behind the stool where Elin sat at the counter. She hadn't fed him, hadn't yet let him out.

"Just a second," she said, flipping through the paper until she found the ad she'd designed for the opening of the PDX Brewpub. A full page, and the colors all true, which wasn't always the case. The logo appeared exactly as she'd intended. But seeing it in the paper made her question the design itself. Was the font too flat, too blocky for the venue? PDX was for hipsters with cash, a watering hole with microbrews, a place for debating banjos, bikes, raising chickens in the city. It was so *Portland*, with its midcentury-modern furniture and walls made of glossy Doug fir logs. The owners had signed off on the logo, had *loved* it, they said, but now Elin didn't trust their instincts. That logo had a whiff of life insurance. Everything about it was wrong.

Fluke whined softly. "Oh. Right," Elin said, but went on sitting, massaging the back of her neck.

Outside the open window the dewy coolness burned off, and another sunny, humidity-free day was on the rise. Ten years, and Elin still wasn't used to Oregon summers, the way she could work for hours under the patio umbrella and still feel energized by day's end. No swelling heat or mugginess weighing her down, no bloodthirsty mosquitoes droning in her ears, sucking her skin into itchy red welts. No alligators in the yard, lizards in the sink, no three o'clock thunderstorms leaving behind a thewy swell of misery. This Pacific Northwest summer of dry air and chirpy little birds and nothing in the yard but tulips and peonies and the neighbor's affectionate tabby.

Goddamn Florida. If she could just figure out why Kate had decided to call after all this time, and then only to talk about the day she'd nearly drowned, then maybe Elin could let it go. But the more Elin had asked about where she'd been and how her daughters were, the more Kate kept on about what it had felt like in those moments before Elin blew the life back inside her. "I must have been dead," she said. "Think about it. Dead."

"I don't want to think about it," Elin had said, wanting to get off the phone. There'd been no love lost between them, but the bad blood, the residual rancor, had caught Elin off guard.

She shut the burner down before the kettle whistled. She needed to call her mother, the last person in the world she felt like talking to.

The metallic green back of a broad-tailed hummingbird caught the sun as it dove into the salvia at the window. Hummingbirds didn't appear very often, especially a broad-tailed with its cricketlike whistling wings, and Rudi called spotting one a *sighting*. He would motion her to the window so they could watch the tiny creatures as furtively as spies through a keyhole. But today Elin rubbed her eyes, hoping that the flash in her head from earlier wasn't a migraine, and for a moment she yearned for winter, for the misty rain and dull overcast perfect for sleeping.

The whistle from the hummingbird's wings traveled through the screen and zapped her forehead with tiny cross-stitches of pain.

She folded the paper closed. The font was fine. Blocky was *bold*. PDX had signed off on it. Loved it. Loved her. She just needed sleep.

It wasn't until the phone rang that she realized how long she'd been staring at the glassy green backsplash above the sink. Lotus, Rudi's receptionist, wanted to know if he'd already left for the dealership.

"Why?" Elin asked. "Is something wrong?"

Lotus didn't answer.

"What is it?"

"It's none of my *business* really. But it's not like I want to work here so bad *anyway*."

The last thing Elin wanted to hear was Lotus's affected rise of intonation as if everything were a question. "I don't have a lot of time this morning," Elin told her. "Rudi will be leaving in a minute—"

"I don't know how to *say* this."

Fluke's claws clicked like glass beads across the tile. Elin opened the screen door and he bolted for the back corner of the yard. "Say what?"

"Well. You remember that time you told Rudi that I deserved a raise for bringing my dad's golfing buddy in? The one who bought the Audi TT?"

"Yes?"

"And how you covered the phone lines for me that time you happened to be here and I had to leave with that *diarrhea thing*?"

"Lotus."

"I guess I just feel like I owe you. I mean, you're such a nice person and I just, well, if I were you I'd want someone to *tell me*?"

Elin's head zinged with a certainty that she should hang up the phone that instant and never speak to this woman again. A before-and-after was about to define Elin's life—she *knew* this—and yet the moment for hanging up was wrestled away by the strength of her own manners, the need to comfort strangers before comforting herself.

Fluke whined at the door. Had he already gone? She let him in and then slumped back onto the stool. "I'm sorry, but I really need to get off the phone."

Fluke leaped onto Elin's lap, the dewy soil from his paws smearing across her robe. She shoved him off, and his ribs thudded against the floor.

"Damn it!" Elin reached for him, but he ran into the next room, and then upstairs and down the hall above her head. "Why are you *calling*, Lotus?"

"Okay! The other day I'm at the counter and this Beemer guy is asking for the owner, you know, he just wants the *owner*, no one else? But I can't find Rudi *anywhere*. And I'm like, looking all over, out in the garage, and he's not there either, and so I go to check the bathroom, the one by the accountant's office. And I knock on the door and I don't hear anything and I'm thinking, *Oh my God*, what if something has happened to him. I heard of this guy once who fainted in the bathroom . . ."

Elin cupped the receiver and called Fluke, whistled softly, but he didn't come.

"And on the way down to the floor he hits his head on the urinal and goes into convulsions and dies right there. So I'm thinking about that guy when I try the bathroom door. Well, I knock, like I said, and I don't hear anything, but it's locked so I go and come back with the key and when I open the door, so, well, there's Poppy, *the girl mechanic*? And she's on top of Rudi who's on top of the toilet and neither of them, you know, has their *pants on*?"

"What's up with him?" Rudi said, appearing in the doorway with Fluke in his arms. "Who's on the phone?"

Elin fumbled the receiver onto its stand. "PDX," she said, her words launched by the banging in her chest, the whole of her insides thrashing. And yet her tone, as clear and calm as if someone else were speaking, prevailed with a purpose she did not quite understand, overcome as she was by a sense that if she could just pull back and hold still the world would not crack in two. "Changed their mind about the logo," she said.

Rudi set Fluke on the floor. "I thought they loved your work," he said, touching her shoulder. Prickly vines unfurled behind her eyes. Another flash of migraine.

His cologne rose like a fence corralling everything in—the passing of his sage-colored dress shirt, fingers through golden hair, chinos swishing socked feet—a collage of a man, arms through a summer jacket, leather shoes cutting across the kitchen, and then a slow, slow face pressing warm lips onto her cool forehead.

"Gotta run," Rudi said, wiping her sweat from his mouth.

Elin closed her robe at her chest. "Early appointment?"

"You don't look well. Are you all right?"

"Headache."

"Should I stay and have breakfast with you?"

Her heart shifted, hard. "Yes," she said. "Why don't you?"

Rudi hesitated, and then sidled onto the stool next to her and grabbed a bran muffin from the bag near the toaster. He didn't remove his jacket.

"I still think you should see another doctor," he said. "A second opinion."

"I've had headaches all my life."

"*Jawohl.* That doesn't make them normal."

Elin clutched a muffin, took a bite, and cleared the choke in her throat. She shook her head, and a feeble laugh she didn't know was there broke loose.

Rudi swallowed. "What?"

She dipped forward in a silent, spastic fit of laughter that produced several tears. She shook her head but her mind would not fall back under her control.

"What?" Rudi asked.

"Kate," she said, finally.

"What about her?"

"On the phone. This reminds me of it."

"*This?*" Rudi glanced at the screen door, his foot bobbing beneath the stool. He took another bite of muffin.

A whole mountain of heartache sat on her chest, making it difficult to breathe. Her mind kept charging toward Kate as if she were the source, the force beneath the unbearable ache. *Should anything happen to me,* Kate had said, *who . . . would look after my girls?* If intended as a dig, it made no sense. *You disappear and then ask such stupid, shithead questions,* Elin had replied. *Where the fuck are you, Kate?*

Elin wiped her runny eyes and fingered the top of her head in search of the side-part, flipping cords of hair where it felt like they belonged. "I think it's a migraine," she said, trying not to squint.

"Sorry?"

Elin stared at his mouth. His German accent made *sorry* sound like *soarey,* like something you couldn't spell in the English language, and the back of her throat filled with disdain—coppery, dry, scratchy as sand.

She coughed. "That's when my headaches started," she said. "That day at the beach." The faded image of Kate's body in the sand appeared like a tarnished photograph in her mind.

"Ah," Rudi said, as if satisfied, as if the story were now told.

The phone rang.

"Don't touch it," Elin said.

"Why?"

"Because I asked you not to."

"O-kaay." Rudi scratched his forehead.

"And don't mock me."

"Who's mocking you?"

The migraine aura filled in the edges of the room with a soft, fleecy violet.

"We need to fix the damn faucet in the master bath," Elin said. "The guy was just here a month ago—we paid him some ungodly sum, and now it's leaking again."

"I hadn't noticed," Rudi said, and glanced at the ringing phone as he slid his jacket off and laid it on the counter.

"Are you serious?" Elin said, and Rudi nodded, his eyes still caught by the phone. "It drips all night," she said. "It keeps me awake."

"That's what you said."

"That *is* what I said." She threw the remainder of her muffin in the sink.

"Okay then."

Elin's cell rang in her purse, which dangled on the coat rack.

"No. It's not okay," Elin said. "That's the point. It's not in any way okay."

Rudi reached for her purse.

"Leave it," she said. And then, "Please."

Rudi stared at the stove, the kettle untouched, the coffee unmade. He stood and took a glass from the cupboard. "Can I get you some juice?"

Elin shook her head. The tiled floor moved in sections like a kaleidoscope. She lifted her eyes to see Rudi's back, his hands, the way they gripped the carton. She imagined yanking at his belt, coming face-to-face with his hard-on. The space behind her eye tightened as if pulled by an invisible wire, and still she couldn't stop herself from wondering what Rudi and Poppy did in that bathroom, *exactly* what they did, and how often, and how long they'd been doing it, and whether it was different from what she and Rudi did at home in what he called their *Ehebett*, their marriage bed, of seven years.

Elin's chest rose for air. She pressed a finger into the bone between her breasts, hard and long, as if corking a hole.

Rudi's phone vibrated in his pocket, each phone going off after the other, a desperate chorus of needs begging them to reenter the outside world of other obligations, other lives. Elin wiped her eyes, one-two, and the aura deepened into a silky, silvery white, one cheek tingling numb. Kate's problem was that she'd never been practical. Not ever. She didn't understand that the only way through a mess was to barrel, smack dab through the middle, as if it had no effect. As if it never happened. "I'll call the guy," Elin said, hopping off her stool.

"I can call him."

"If he thinks he can charge me," she said.

"I said I'll call him."

"No." Elin pulled the bag of kibble from the lower cabinet and filled Fluke's bowl, adding an extra scoop for making him wait, for knocking him to the floor, while feeling Rudi rigid and tall as a maypole at her back.

"You should go to bed," he said.

"I was thinking the same."

"Before it gets worse."

"Yes," she said, and nudged the bowl with her foot as Fluke gorged, just to see if he'd growl. Just to see if he'd bite as he stumbled after it. Elin stopped, and then she nudged it again.

Rudi came up from behind, turned her around.

"Don't touch me," she meant to say. "Don't," right there in the curl of her tongue, where it stayed as her cheek tingled against his collarbone, words dissolving into the purple patina around her head.

FOUR

THE CARDBOARD BOXES STACKED AGAINST the wall were decades old and soft as suede to the touch. Vivvie carefully shoved as many as she could lift up onto the closet shelf while balancing atop a stepladder in the spare bedroom. If she came crashing down Averlee would have to call 911 again, and the awful possibility was like a rope holding Vivvie stable above the girls drinking Pepsis on the floor below her. From this high up their white curls appeared like cotton wigs in the heat. In an instant her house had become another planet—slurpy little elves underfoot, bare toes swishing across her kitchen floor like whispers.

The window unit sputtered cool air, but a dampness remained, especially after Vivvie stripped away the musty blankets and drapes, now knocking the drum inside the washing machine across the hall. The air smelled faintly of bleach.

It was nearly lunchtime in Florida and still no word from Elin. Surely she was up by now. Vivvie had left three messages on both of Elin's phones. *Call me, call me, call me.*

Averlee reached into a box of plastic knickknacks and pulled out a set of speckled pink poodles. Quincy found the porcelain pigs with the black bows that Kate had painted sloppily on their heads during summer camp when she was around Quincy's age. For years the pigs had been arranged from largest to smallest on the kitchen windowsill until Kate hit adolescence and declared them the dumbest, most embarrassing things she'd ever seen. She raged at Vivvie for having placed them there, for liking something so stupid, and Vivvie found herself defending the ugly pigs against her daughter, clutching them to her chest, and then, in the end, carefully packing them away, like Fabergé eggs, in the box her granddaughters now opened.

"Once I get this room all straightened up I don't want to find a thing thrown down in here," Vivvie said, sweating as she stepped off the ladder with a box of photographs that wouldn't fit.

The girls said nothing, not now, not most of the morning.

Vivvie set the box on the bed. "Averlee, why don't you go ahead and pull your stuff out of that grocery bag and put it in the bottom drawer." Vivvie pointed to the oak dresser. "Put yours to one side and Quincy's on the other."

Averlee plopped the whole bag inside the drawer.

"That's not what I said."

The girl leaned back on her heels and stared.

"What? Are we having some kind of standoff, you and me?" Vivvie wiped her forehead.

Quincy scooted in front of Averlee and emptied two striped shirts and three pairs of khaki shorts into the heavy drawer. Unlike what they were wearing, the clothes in the drawer had seen better days. A frayed shirt hem, pockets worn white along the edge.

"You two are going to need some more clothes," Vivvie said.

"How long are we going to be here?" Averlee asked.

Vivvie didn't answer.

"And what do we call you?"

Sunlight caught the dark flecks in Averlee's light eyes. Elin's eyes. Jackson's before hers.

Vivvie sat on the bed. *What should they call her?* She was no different than a neighbor lady, a stranger who could have sold them candy at Roth's. She was Mrs. Fenton, an old woman living alone in a house at the end of a street. "I'm your grandma," she said, but that was just a hollow fact. "So . . . *Grandma* will do." She massaged her jaw. "We'll have to see about the rest."

Averlee pursed her lips, keeping whatever thoughts she was having to herself. The washing machine whined and thunked to a stop, deepening the sudden silence.

"Are you done with that Pepsi?" Vivvie asked.

Averlee jiggled the empty can.

Was it considered rude these days, jiggling a can instead of answering your grandmother? Kids did and said all sorts of things at Roth's while their parents poked at cell phones, glancing up just long enough to ask if pulling candy off a shelf or fighting with a sister or hitting their own mother was a good choice or a bad choice.

Vivvie rose from the bed. "Put the can in the bag of empties under the sink," she said.

Averlee leaned on her heels again, and after a moment seemed to think better of whatever she'd had in mind, and headed toward the kitchen with the can.

Vivvie carved out extra space in the bottom of the closet, and it was only then that she noticed her old jewelry box on its side, a wooden creaky thing held together by a rusted hinge at the back, a single latch clasped shut at the front. The smell of cedar rose when she opened it. The colorful beaded necklace Elin had made for her in the third grade lay on top in a tangle. Beneath it a scatter of cheap bangles Vivvie's mother left behind when she died, and there was Kate's baby bracelet from the hospital. At the very bottom lay Vivvie's wedding band, thinner than she remembered, the gold turned on the inside from her skin, a part of her left there for decades.

She spun it around her knuckle, but it was made for a younger hand. She wedged, and pulled taut her finger, but the ring would not budge, and she finally slid it off and returned it to the box.

Averlee stood in the doorway, watching. "Quincy's feeling better," she said.

Vivvie stuffed the jewelry box behind a larger box in the closet, and added another on top like a barricade. "Well, good. That's good," she said. "Did you put the can where it belongs?"

"Yes."

"Thank you," Vivvie said, feeling the girl's eyes still on her even after her back was turned.

FIVE

THE CONCRETE PILINGS BENEATH THE house allowed for the pounding feet inside to echo past the floorboards all the way out into the yard. Vivvie could hear the girls' laughter, too, could tell they were playing some game.

A trail of confederate jasmine ran wild up the telephone pole to the rear of the side lawn, and every morning Vivvie watered and sniffed and pinched away dried buds. But it was nearly noon, too hot to water, too hot *not to*, and hurrying through the wet heat with sugary perfume around her head made her feel a little sick. She shut the hose down and grabbed the broom from the porch.

In her imaginings their reunion was always filled with hugs and apologies, softhearted as they'd never been in real life. But Vivvie's arms felt heavy at the thought of wrapping them around her own daughter. The vision of Kate's bloodless face and wasted body was now the only vision she seemed to own of her daughter, the rest of their lives erased, and to touch that woman in the hospital bed was to break her in half, kill her dead on the spot.

She swept the sandy soil from the walkway, needing a cigarette as bad as she'd ever needed one in her life, but the tiny voices springing from the house made her want to quit, turned the act of smoking into some kind of disgrace. She'd never felt that way with her own daughters, never hesitated to fill her insides with tar when they were around.

The bristles jammed against clumps of grass invading the walkway, the mowing and edging clearly past due. Wink took care of both yards and Vivvie made a mental note to knock on his door when he got home. She made another note to spare him the details about Kate.

She halted the broom, listened for the phone, heard nothing, and in the absence of ringing felt the flimsy line connecting her to Elin, recalling the postcard she sent Vivvie years ago with a picture of Mount Hood. *Living above sea level with snowcapped mountains like a Hollywood backdrop in the sky. And guess what? I married a German man. Happy.* She drew a smiley face and signed it, *Elin.* A postcard. For a wedding announcement. To her mother.

Two years later, Kate left with Averlee and Quincy, claiming she just had to get out, claiming there were things Vivvie was incapable of understanding. "Try me," Vivvie had said, but Kate told her not to worry. Told her every town was in need of a good waitress. Told her she would be in touch once she settled. "Settled *where?*" Vivvie asked. "I'll let you know," Kate said, but Vivvie already sensed she never would. That evening Vivvie couldn't seem to rise from her porch swing, entranced by the west, the direction her other daughter had taken. The skinny red bark of pines sliced up the sunset, the row of deep green treetops hovered like summits above the glow, as beautiful a sight as Vivvie would ever see, and the splendor filled her with a bottomless dread.

A howl from inside the house, a breathless giggle, as if someone were being tickled, tingled Vivvie's chest. Her insides buttered up as if she might laugh and cry all together.

She fanned her blouse and swept until the end of the walkway. The hum of Wink's truck caused her to look up, but instead of seeing Wink across the yard, Vivvie came face-to-face with a snake dangling from the pecan tree, a snake so black it was blue.

She jerked back and cocked the broomstick, her body filled with the heat of rage. The truck door slammed and Wink crossed the yard toward her, a stuffed Roth's Grocery bag in hand. "What the hell's going on down there at Roth's?" he called out. "Things are a mess when you're off work."

"Get back," she said, hoisting the broom higher.

He followed her line of sight. "I'll be damned. That's an indigo," he said. "A five-thousand-dollar fine if you swing that broom."

"So you're the game warden now?"

"No, ma'am."

"I can't have it this close to the house."

"It ain't even full grown."

"And never will be."

"Vivvie."

"I can't stand a snake," she said, and swung as if the snake were a piñata, whipping the creature to the ground. It appeared stunned, its head lifting and falling while the rest of it spun as if searching for the ground underneath.

Vivvie dropped the broom and ran for a trowel in the bucket of gardening tools on the porch.

"The hell now," Wink said.

She rushed up on the snake as if wielding a bowie knife. One whip and the trowel's tip made a deep sucking sound when it pinned the Indigo to the spongy grass—a fraction from splitting the thing in two.

Wink drew an elbow to his face. "Good Christ, Vivvie." The twisty snake ends flipped and whirled in the bloodstained grass like sidewinders in a fight.

Sweat glued Vivvie's blouse to her skin. "I can't stand a snake."

"You could have called someone."

"Is that right."

"Yes, it is."

"People waiting by the phone when a black snake dangles in your face?"

"There are people who take them away. Or something," he said.

Vivvie crouched to inspect under her truck and porch, and even though it was too far to see, the crawlspace beneath her steps. "If there's one there's bound to be another."

"I wouldn't advise going under there."

"I'm not scared."

"Clearly."

Vivvie stood. "The grass is too long."

Wink studied the yard. "What are you saying?"

"The grass is too long."

"That's what I heard you say, but I suspect you mean something else."

"Well."

"You think the snake showed up because the grass is too long?"

"Your words, not mine."

"Besides, it was hanging from a branch in your tree. Maybe you need to trim your tree back."

Vivvie tipped her head to the side.

The snake lay motionless now, flies already buzzing above it.

Wink removed his glasses and rubbed his eyes. He replaced them and held up the grocery bag, his face sunburned, his pants baggy, his button-down shirt hanging at least a size too big from his skinny shoulders, reminding her of the waving, inflatable tube man outside the Ford dealership. "Like I was saying," he said. "There were only two cashiers, one slow-poking as bad as the other. Lines backed all the way up to the baby food at one end, produce at the other." He nodded in easterly and westerly directions.

Vivvie studied both their yards and up into the trees.

"How come you're off today?" Wink asked. "Your schedule change?"

"Something like that."

"You all right there, Vivvie?"

She breathed heavily through her nose. "What do you think?"

He was already turned, staring at her house. "Don't look now, but you've got little people in your windows," he said.

"Ah, hell," Vivvie said.

"Where'd they come from?"

"Probably saw the whole thing."

"The way their eyes are bugging. Yeah."

Time was playing tricks again—the humor in Wink's voice, or maybe just the heat—but in that moment she missed Jackson so bad it hurt her throat.

She wandered up to the porch swing and plopped herself down. Wink joined her, the weight of him slight, but heavy enough to start them swinging. He smelled like salty popcorn, and his shirt, line-dried and stiff, called to mind her mother's clean sheets, her childhood with cherry taffy and colas in the heat. She'd had a tire swing, and in that same oak tree a playhouse her father built just for her. All those hours spent with her head hung out the door, gazing through the dense leaves, clouds swelling together or tearing apart in the blue. She hid from the rain up there, dreamed of becoming a teacher and a mother like her own mother, who wore pressed yellow dresses and on the weekends shared pretty drinks with her father at Jake's Crab House down the street. Vivvie's husband was going to be a man like her father, a man who kept her daughters laughing. A man who lived into ripe and tender old age.

The girls were no longer at the window, no longer laughing or padding the floors. Just Vivvie and Wink swinging side by side, widow and widower gnawed by memories, though his were surely nothing like hers.

SIX

ELIN LAY IN THE SHADY grass next to Fluke near Rudi's garden. She rubbed her temple and flipped, dopily, through a copy of *Inside the World of Insects*. Instead of her usual Parisian-style skirt and leggings, she wore loose khaki shorts, a yellow T-shirt with *Keep Portland Weird* on the front, and her biggest, darkest pair of sunglasses. Her migraine meds had barely begun to kick in.

Rudi had tilled the garden in early spring and the chicken manure still tinged the rich soil, its smell rising now and then, causing Fluke's nose to quiver and run with the breeze. Elin was determined to read through the tunnel of her one-eyed headache. It wouldn't be the first time. She had work to do, an entire branding campaign for the new insect exhibit at the Oregon Zoo. But words kept sliding around the page, snippets about small pests scrabbling from their burrows, sucking the life out of everything. She imagined the creaky sound of grubs twisting the roots of the garden, and then a brackish gumbo of ruin in their wake. Another wave of nausea passed through her.

She set the book on her chest and squinted at the polarized sky. Tree branches shot across the cadet-blue like veins. The medication made her drowsy, and for a split second she forgot about Poppy and the call from Kate. A moment later she remembered, and it hit her even harder when it returned.

Her mother had left three messages this morning—*Call me, call me, call me*, gurgling like an old percolator inside Elin's head. Kate must have gotten hold of her, too. A goddamn reunion! Hip fucking hurray.

Elin didn't mean that. She cared about her little sister on some level, surely she did, surely they'd been close before their father died, if only by the logic of circumstances—*all's well until tragedy strikes!* But it wasn't as if she possessed a cache of "better times" memories as proof that she and her sister had once gotten along. All she had was a vague glimpse of a five- and four-year-old at the Strawberry Festival, faces painted by a hippie girl with a thin, cold brush. And then their mother kneeling all the way down to take Elin and Kate into her arms at the same time. They peered at one another behind their mother's hair, Kate's cheeks dappled in butterflies, ladybugs, and rainbows, her lips the slick, bloodred stain of berries. Elin smiled at her, and Kate smiled back, revealing a row of glossy red teeth. Elin ran her tongue across her own teeth. They would be red, too, her cheeks covered in the same colors and shapes as Kate's, her hairline smeared with the same sweaty wisps of hair. They were mirrors of each other, and being reflected in her sister's face had stayed with Elin, a strange and simple affection, woven of connective tissue, inborn, easy, a natural joy.

But no matter. That was all there was. Whatever they had been to one another all those years ago was not enough to sustain them for all that came after. Elin simply couldn't stand Kate. Not her scratchy voice, not her off-key humor, not her temper, not her arrogance over wearing secondhand clothes, not her bizarre decision to disappear, and certainly not her choice in men. When would she ever grow up? And yet Elin could never quite free herself of the guilty feeling that her sister somehow *belonged* to her, like a child given up for adoption, willingly abandoned by a mother who preferred never to lay eyes on her again. And in this same way the mere thought of Kate was enough to make Elin feel bad about herself.

Elin had been annoyed by Kate's phone call, sure, but she'd been relieved, too. Hadn't she? To know, in the very least, that her sister was alive, and her nieces, even though she'd never laid eyes on them, were okay, too? It didn't hurt too badly to let the truth of that in. It was just that no one could infuriate Elin the way Kate could. No one else in her life had ever made her want to throw a punch, and then actually *throw one*, besides Kate.

Until now.

"I was such a good nephew to my Tante Inge," Rudi had whispered to Elin in bed right after Kate's call. They'd been discussing families, though neither lived within a thousand miles of a single relative. "Coffee and *Kuchen* every Sunday, while listening to Tante Inge talk about her *Kreislaufstoerung*." He laughed. "But I *did* love her, and in the end she left me a nice inheritance, which brought me to the States, and then I found you." He kissed the tip of her nose. "Family is important. My cousin Gerti was a widow raising seven children alone and couldn't have done it without help from aunts and uncles and grandparents. All of Gerti's kids turned out to be a success." Elin could see his smile in the moonlight. What exactly had been his point? That families were essential to happiness? That they saved us all from failure? He was her family. He was her happiness, his background so markedly different from hers that even after seven years he remained a constant conduit to another world, a bottomless box of discovery into a language she couldn't speak, to politicians, pop singers, and actors she'd never heard of, to exotic meats and aged cheeses and almond sweets she'd never before tasted until Rudi brought them home from the new specialty shop in the neighborhood and shared with her the flavor of his fairytale childhood. But she'd stopped listening to his talk about family. In that moment it was nothing but a rude reminder of Kate, of her mother, of the fact that where Elin came from the good life was defined under very different terms.

Rudi loved his siblings and his cousins—engineers, architects, dentists, and accountants, as if each relative had chosen a profession by tracing a finger down the list of career choices in a high school handout. He'd been going on about the architect and some building in Berlin, but Elin was searching for Rudi's smile in the dark, no longer visible; she'd always loved his full red lips, the way they reminded her, oddly, yet erotically, of Ingrid Bergman's, surrounding the most beautiful white teeth she'd ever seen. His mouth always so fresh and clean, strangely savory, and this must have been what she was imagining when she'd finally fallen asleep.

Now she lay in the grass thinking of all the lies inside Rudi's mouth, like a black swarm of flies feeding off his tongue.

She massaged her forehead, propped the book back up on her chest, but couldn't read. On their third date Rudi told her she seemed too "patrician" to come from the family she'd described, and when he said this he studied her hair and eyes, the scarf around her neck. She loved hearing him say that. It confirmed what she'd believed all along, that she didn't belong to those people, and never had. Instead of connecting Elin with her past, Rudi had marveled at the way she'd pulled herself out of it like a diamond from the rough. She was the sparkly gem he protected with an umbrella on the street after dinner, whispering that he was falling in love with her, and she whispered the same. Maybe the rain tapping the umbrella, the steam rising from wet concrete, the fine Pinot Noir warming their blood, had all served as a setting for love, a mood mistaken for the thing itself, romancing them into believing in each other when they were really nothing more than actors caught up in a scene. Maybe one had believed and the other had not.

THINGS WE SET ON FIRE

Seven years they'd been married. The seven-year itch. Was Poppy Rudi's itch? Elin searched for a clue that something had been off, revealed in increments over time, like tiny fissures, virtually unnoticeable but for the cumulative effect on the whole. All right. There was a loneliness, a silence that had crept into the bathroom after they made love, the way they no longer looked at one another beneath the vanity light, just wiped themselves clean, no laughter, no bite on the shoulder in the mirror while the shuddering was still warm, still throbbing beneath their skin.

She sucked in a breath, nausea gaining on her. A giant pulse inside her skull burned hot and cold as frostbite.

Maybe those fissures, that silence was nothing more than a settling in—maybe it was all just *marriage*, the way in which it worked.

What did she know of marriage? It had always felt a little like playing house. Rudi practicing "husbandry" in his plastic clogs, spading up the soil, watering and pruning with that effeminate European air, which frankly, Elin didn't care for. And did he care for her in an apron, potting daisies along the patio? On a stepladder, hanging pressed linen drapes in the long French windows? She listened with practiced patience while he spoke of BMWs and then he did the same while she spoke of articles in *Adbusters* magazine, and they shared more Pinot over pesto pasta as the evening breeze filled the dining room with the sweetness of honeysuckle they'd planted, together, along the length of the cedar fence.

She recalled the odd bruises on his elbows from months ago, spotted beneath his short sleeves when his hands were submerged in the dishes at the sink. And what had he told her? "Must have happened when I tripped over a part in the service department." She'd laughed. "Poor baby," she'd said, kissing his cheek. Kissing him for hurting himself during bathroom trysts on the floor, his elbows grinding into grout between the tiny white tiles, his dick in Poppy's mouth, or deep through the center of her, their red mouths suctioning one another until jerking loose, in need of air, of letting go a scream. Elin kissing his cheek for all those long hours, starting early, finishing late. "You look a little tired." Kiss. What a diamond Poppy must be under her slate-blue jumpsuit, and beyond that, her brain chock-full of the workings of German engines. "Business is booming," Rudi told her not long ago. "In this economy?" Elin had asked, feeling happy for him, relieved. Kiss. "Crazy," he said. "I know."

Elin rolled her head to the side, the garden a profusion of shape and color, a glutted showroom, a county fair competition. Of all the headaches she'd ever had, this one had to be the worst.

She glanced at the page in front of her. *Their mouthparts are shaped like hypodermic needles, which they use to pierce the tender plants and siphon out their juices.*

She tossed the book into the grass and peered through rows of bright round tomatoes, slick peppers, cucumbers next to the wildly open spray of rosemary, lavender, and sage. By now her migraine prescription should have fully kicked in. *Topamax helps you live again.* A bullshit ad campaign. The yard beyond the garden resembled a purple Easter card fade-out, the shapes of the vegetables an orgy of colorful, overlapping balls.

She forced herself to stand, even as the ground shifted beneath her. A bubble belched free of her stomach. She tiptoed to the antiqued cabinet on the patio as if trying not to wake her own mind. Fluke followed, sniffing her ankles, then jumping back as if sensing a threat, a murderous smell to her skin. Elin lifted a trowel from the drawer. "Go," she said, and Fluke sat in place, looking up at her, not in defiance, but because she hadn't clarified where she meant for him to be.

She kneeled in the shifting shade, breeze in her hair, the greens and blues and whites of the plants and flowers, the cries of jays vying for the trees, all dancing on the edge of a magenta aura like some hallucinogenic dream.

The musky soil, the scent of Rudi's hands, rose to her face, as she stabbed a cucumber in half. Fluke scrambled when Elin swung again. She should have known better than to get married. Women in her family didn't have marriages. They had tragedies, mishaps, fiery connections to men and to the memories of men, one outdoing the next. Her father, killed in what should have been an avoidable hunting accident, if he'd only worn the proper vest, but instead decided to blend with the forest, merge into his very own death, leaving Elin and Kate with a resentful widow for a mother, a woman who wouldn't know love if it crawled into her lap and licked her face. And Kate's joke of a marriage to Neal, *Neal*, whose own failed-love history reverberated like an earthquake beneath Elin's feet. The two of them a bona fide eight-point disaster. Christ. Neal was the last person she wanted to think about now. No need to go anywhere near that mess to locate her own failings in life because after all these years of believing she had left it behind, convinced herself she was immune, or rather *cured* of the past and its mistakes, Elin had ended up with a championship tragedy all her own.

Her hands shook as she hacked the waxy vegetables, ripped the greens, swung and flailed until the gelatinous insides of fleshy tomatoes oozed like bloody snot between her fingers.

When she stopped, her head hurt so badly that she wondered if she'd accidentally stabbed her own skull. She came to her feet, dizzy and nauseous, one eye closed as she gazed through a peacock-blue tunnel surrounded by swing-back lawn chairs, a stainless steel grill, potted daisies on the brick patio.

She let go the vomit that had been threatening all morning.

Fluke came running. She spit her mouth clean and dropped the trowel, caught her breath, and lifted Fluke to her cheek, felt his quick heart thumping against her bone. She kissed his forehead, placed him back on the grass, and then fumbled her way inside the house and down the stairs into the basement.

Skis and extra lawn chairs passed the edges of her vision like wheat in the wind. She caught her balance on the stacked boxes of Rudi's childhood paraphernalia—stamp and coin collections, children's books about giant geese and wolves and a child with scissors for hands.

In the storage room against the wall, Rudi had organized the luggage into rows of neat pyramids, large on bottom, medium in the middle, and small on top. Elin yanked the largest from the bottom, and the rest tumbled to the floor.

The phone rang as she dragged the suitcase upstairs and through the kitchen. Fluke paced between the stools and her feet, then ran to his bowl and sniffed. There was no hand signal she could give him to help him understand.

Elin released the luggage and tottered in place. It was as if she'd stepped into the ocean, waves pulling her one way then another. She lifted the suitcase again but dropped it, the plastic handle hitting the tile with a loud pop. Fluke shot down the hall, and the phone seemed to have stopped ringing and then started again. Elin squeezed her grimy hands into fists before reaching for the handset. "What?" she said, smelling soil, peppers, vomit. "*What?*"

Her mother's voice was saying *Kate. Hospital. Girls. These girls. Pepsi. A snake.*

"I need you to come," her mother said, her scratchy voice so much like Kate's, breaking through as if the volume were suddenly turned way too high.

Elin tried twice to say, "No. I'm already *going* somewhere," but the words just would not come.

SEVEN

AVERLEE COULD SEE THE BOTTOM was about to fall out of the box her grandmother was lifting off the bed, but she had no time to say so before an avalanche of photographs broke free and spilled to the floor near Averlee's knees.

"Son of a bitch," her grandmother said, grappling an arm underneath until she finally gave up and tossed the collapsed box back onto the bed. "Sorry," she said. "I forgot you two were here."

She kneeled on the floor, stared at the mess, and then held up a photo for them to see. Her hand was red-knuckled, green veins twisting across the top. She smelled like cigarettes. "Do you recognize that girl right there?" she said. "That's your mother at the beach with your aunt Elin."

Averlee studied the picture. The girls were the size of her and Quincy, squinting against the sun. Stringy hair and long towels hung from their shoulders; the ocean filled the space behind their legs.

Quincy leaned in for a look.

Their grandmother leaned, too. She said, "See how Averlee favors your aunt Elin in the eyes and mouth? You see, Averlee?"

It was true, like squinting back at herself. Averlee had never seen a picture of her mother as a girl, and she couldn't take her eyes off this miniature version, like a plastic figurine from one of Quincy's shelves. Last night Averlee had poked her mother's arm at the kitchen table, causing her head to wobble toward the row of orange pill bottles. It was dark, only the street lamp along the curtain's edge to see what was before her, and Averlee had waited for her mother to move, the refrigerator humming loudly at her back. She did not turn on the light.

"That's *Mommy* in this picture?" Quincy asked.

"So you *can* talk after all," their grandmother said.

Quincy wiped her nose on the back of her hand.

The air conditioner sputtered and a frosty chill stung the sweat on Averlee's neck.

Quincy traced their mother's long hair in the photograph. "I don't get it," she said to Averlee. "That's you in the picture with Mommy."

"Weren't you listening? Don't be silly," Averlee said.

"I'm not silly."

"How could that be me in a picture with Mommy when she was little?"

"It looks like you."

"She says it's Mommy's sister." Averlee gestured a hand toward their grandmother but didn't turn to look at her.

A heavy quiet lay like a coat across Averlee's back.

"I prefer 'Grandma' to 'she,'" her grandmother said, in a voice so much like her own mother's, so much like the one she used months ago when, instead of asking Averlee to light a match for her, she tried over and over until she lit one herself at the sink, but never turned to light the candle on the counter. The fire burned down to her mother's finger, and when Averlee touched her arm, the match flew into the drain and her mother said, "For God'sssssssake. For. God's . . ." Her perfume hung in the kitchen long after she'd closed herself up in her bedroom.

"Can we look at all of them?" Quincy asked.

THINGS WE SET ON FIRE

"I don't see why not," their grandmother said as she gathered the photographs back onto the bed. She checked her watch. "I need to see if I can get that aunt of yours to answer her phone." She stood as if waiting for Averlee and Quincy to speak.

They didn't, and now the room felt strangely empty without their grandmother rattling in the corners. They had been here before. Averlee couldn't place it exactly, but the mix of cigarettes and coffee, the rose-scented air freshener was familiar. The cookie jar shaped like a clock on the kitchen counter. She had seen it, tasted lemon wafers from inside it. They had been here before they had enough words to remember it by.

And now she'd left them alone. But it wasn't her grandmother Averlee missed. It was the braided rug in her bedroom at home, smelling like the cherry sucker Quincy broke between her teeth and let fall like slivers of red glass between the seams.

Her grandmother's voice carried down the hall. "Hospital . . . Snake . . . *These girls.*"

Averlee liked to flop onto her belly and read on that rug. She liked the sound of wasps floating to and from a nest outside her window, sometimes ticking the glass as if the heat were too much, even for them. The book she hadn't finished was still there, one of the things she'd meant to grab when the police said they had to go, but she forgot as soon as Quincy started to cry. Now she wondered if they were ever going home, if she would ever find out what happened at the end of that series. Neighbors becoming werewolves, cheerleaders turned into vampires, a teacher turned zombie on the weekends. What Averlee hated about those books was what she loved. By the end, none of those things would turn out to be true.

Quincy placed the photographs across the bed until they resembled rooms in a house, some long and dark, others square and bright. Familiar-looking strangers filled each one.

Before today Averlee had never known she'd had other relatives besides her grandmother, who'd disappeared long ago like her father, and her aunt Elin, whom she'd never seen at all. Now their grandmother was back, and Averlee held in her hand a picture of a man who resembled her mother, his hair parted with the same twist and dip, his tooth a little crooked in the same small way in the bottom front row behind the same pouty lip. He swung a girl by her wrists, and her long hair flung through the air, her bare feet flying as if she were a baby, but she wasn't. She couldn't have been much younger than Quincy was now. That swinging girl was Averlee's mother.

"Who do you think they are?" Quincy asked over her shoulder.

The thought of her mother having a daddy who swung her by her wrists caused a sharp pain in Averlee's head. "Don't know," she said, and lifted an old-timey snapshot of a woman with a baby in her lap. Another of a man with a mule. They didn't resemble anyone she knew.

Quincy turned over the photograph of the man swinging the girl, pointing out something in pencil across the back. "I can't read the cursive," she said.

When Averlee didn't say anything, Quincy patted her hand the way their mother used to, and just like their mother, she said, "It's never as bad as you think, Ave."

Down the hall their grandma said, "Well. That may be. But that was *then*. What on earth do you expect me to do *now*?"

"Jackson," Averlee read to Quincy from the photograph. "And his baby girl."

Averlee hopped off the bed and imitated her mother's zombie walk all the way into the living room, a sad-looking limp from when she could at least still walk.

This was the house her mother had grown up in but never talked about. Maybe that was where she sat and watched TV, on a sofa the color of an apricot with matching chairs. Maybe the bubbly light strung on a chain was what she read by. And all those gold-framed paintings of lakes and barns, the ugly brown drapes, the line of glass elephants next to a ball of hairy yarn on a shelf. Maybe all things that her mother had once touched, or even owned.

Averlee shifted her hip, made the bad leg worse.

"Still. You don't sound right," her grandmother said into the phone. "Are you having one of those headaches?"

Averlee dragged herself to the front door, where she stared out the window past the screened porch into the yard next door, at the neighbor's red truck. Then she realized she was pretending with the wrong leg and switched her weight and lumbered to the picture window, pulling her foot across the carpet, which wasn't quite right but she liked the way the fibers folded into a dark line behind her heel.

"Hold on," her grandmother said into the phone. "Is something wrong with your leg?" she called out.

Averlee turned.

"What in the Sam Hill is wrong with your leg?"

EIGHT

ELIN COULD HAVE FLOWN TO Central Florida and arrived within hours, but the idea of a road trip held for her a kind of hope, a chance to see some country, to clear her head of love, of the question of love. A *journey* instead of a trip, instead of a rescue, instead of sticking her dog in a cargo crate and shipping him in subnormal temperatures at thirty thousand feet above the earth.

"Are you ready for our journey?" she asked Fluke, who turned, skeptically, from the backseat window where he'd been peering out toward their house. Elin hit the gas and knocked him onto the pebbled leather.

It took several days on the road for her headache to completely dissolve. But in its place a groggy weight, like a sloshy bladder of wine behind her eyes, tipped her balance if she moved too quickly while rising from the car to fill her gas tank, or use the bathroom, or lean against the car while Fluke ran circles in a patch of grass. Steady, while checking into hotels that smelled of cigarettes and gas station pastries. Careful, while drinking thin, tasteless coffee, heat rising, humidity worming her hair, hands grimy no matter how many times she squirted the pungent minimart cleansers into her palm, but finally, finally, the headache left her alone.

Other than Rudi, she told no one she was leaving, and him by leaving a handwritten note near the phone. *Enjoy Poppy* was all it said. Of the twenty-two messages Rudi had left on her cell in three days, she hadn't listened to a single one.

The updates from her mother about Kate had hit a dead end. Kate was awake, this much they knew, but knew only because she was refusing visitors, including her own mother. It was just like her to be so rotten, even at a time like this. The staff wouldn't release any information, other than to confirm that Kate was still there. It had been three days.

In the meantime, Elin's life streamed behind her like a kite—answering work emails at rest stops, shipping her ideas into the Oregon ether at her back. The scenery she'd wanted to lose herself in turned out to be little more than a soft smudge at the edge of her vision—from the red mountains of Arizona to the rust-colored Texas plains—but that was fine, just as well, all that beauty made her uneasy. Every spark of pleasure was crippled by a tender torment. Her affection for Fluke drove her mind straight to Poppy. To feel love, even dog-love, was to imagine Rudi in the bathroom with Elin at home, Rudi in the bathroom with Poppy at work. Elin could do without the purple mountains. She was grateful that between the amber fields and sapphire lakes, miles of dull, chaotic sprawl filled the country in.

Her wagon was filthy from Louisiana rain, and by the time she reached the golden sunshine of northern Florida the windows were so spattered with lovebugs that everything inside, including Elin, was cast against dozens of splotchy shadows.

At dusk on the fourth day she pulled into the driveway of the Whistling Willows Bed and Breakfast, just east of Orlando. With her nieces in her mother's spare room, Elin was free, thankfully, to stay where she liked. Her hips ached and her legs gave slightly as she rose into the soupy air that smelled of oranges and freshly cut grass. She braced a hand against the sizzling car, and drew it back. Crusty insects chipped off beneath her fingers. Their acidic bodies would wreak havoc on the paint.

She'd forgotten how thick and deeply green the leaves grew, how solidly the trees gripped the earth. Everywhere orange and red blossoms were shooting throughout the year.

She wiped her fingers on the rear of her shorts and studied the house—a milky, placid manor hemmed in on three sides by what the Internet claimed was one of the few remaining orange groves in Central Florida. Enormous white pillars of a Greek-revival portico, a long wooden porch shaded by ancient live oaks, all set against the expanse of a manicured lawn. Two weeping willows drooped along the stone walkway. The horizon glowed an unnatural orange-red through dangling oranges, the entire scene a giant mural of the South.

The oval placard at the end of the driveway read PETS WELCOME in fine, loopy script. Beneath that—SMOKERS ARE NOT. It was August and the heat trapped inside the blacktop penetrated Elin's thin leather soles. She opened the passenger door and Fluke leaped into the grass, where he immediately lifted a leg, peed on a row of bright pink azaleas, and then ventured across the yard. Elin had left Florida nearly a decade ago without any intention of returning, but here was her beloved Oregon dog scratching his back in thick Saint Augustine grass beneath a giant oak draped in moss, and the whole scene so disoriented her that she yanked the suitcase from the wagon just to feel in charge.

"You must be Elin!" a voice called out. The large oak door stood open, and a trim, dark-haired woman, late fifties perhaps, said, "Welcome, welcome, come on in." She scooped the air above her head as she came off the porch and cut across the yard.

"I'm guessing you're Marianne Mayes," Elin said.

"I am just that, but everybody calls me Shug, like sugar, don't ask me why. Goes back so far I don't even know how it got started." Her handshake was strong as a man's. "You need some help with your things there?"

"No, thank you. I've only got the one suitcase. Short trip." She closed the tailgate. "That's Fluke, by the way, making himself at home."

"Hey, boy," Shug said, patting her thighs.

Fluke stopped and shook his head, before taking off to sniff the next tree.

"Well. Oregon," Shug said, as if it were Elin's name.

Elin wiped the sweat around her nose.

"I had a cousin moved out there when her husband wanted to get into the seed-growing business, if you can imagine a notion like that. Didn't matter anyway cause they turned right back around after six months. Couldn't stand all that rain. Said it liked to never let up."

Sweat dribbled down Elin's scalp and around her ears. Less than five minutes in the heat and already her cotton blouse clung to her chest. "It does get pretty wet in the winter," she said. "But if you're patient enough summer comes around like nothing you've ever seen."

"Well, if you're patient enough anything's bound to come around sooner or later."

Elin released the handle of her luggage and whistled sharply with her fingers. Fluke jumped to his feet and ran to her side.

If Shug was impressed with his training she didn't show it. She led them into the house and up the winding oak staircase to the second floor. "Here's your key, darlin'. Breakfast is at eight if that's all right with you." She kneeled and scratched under Fluke's chin. "Righty roo," she said, and was gone.

Elin rolled her luggage next to the brass bed, where Fluke had already stretched out beneath a spinning ceiling fan. She was surprised to find herself charmed by the Southern kitsch. Handmade dolls on a chest of drawers. Black-and-white portraits of families from another century hung in neat little tiers of lace frames on the rose-colored walls. Ducks, hearts, a doily beneath the Lord's Prayer carved into a block of wood on the nightstand. Next to that, a frosted bowl of hard candies.

Elin fell back onto the quilt, patted Fluke's hip, and closed her eyes but felt as if she were still driving, the whole country zooming west to east, traveling back in time. She opened her eyes and the fan made it worse. Not just the movement, but the way it filled the room with the smell of warm cedar windowpanes, so familiar that Elin sat up, recalling her mother at the dinner table, the two of them watching a plate of pork chops lose their steam, a bowl of sweet potatoes curling into their skins. Kate was crying down the hall on the other side of the bathroom door. Fourteen years old, crying that she was going to use a razor. She meant it, she said, she was going to use that razor on herself right now. She beat what sounded like her fists on the edge of the sink. The ceiling fan spun above the table.

Elin stayed put with her mother, unable to move. Kate had never before threatened to do such a thing.

Vivvie finally slapped her palms onto the table, shoved her chair back, walked with an unfamiliar slow measure, and banged once on the bathroom door. "Knock off your damn foolishness and get to the dinner table," she said.

Kate immediately quit crying.

"I mean it," Vivvie said. "You aren't half as crazy as you'd have us believe. Now get out here. Dinner's getting cold."

To Elin's surprise, Kate swung open the door, her face puffed red and wet when she sat down at the table. She didn't look up, just slung sweet potatoes and forked a pork chop onto her plate, and started eating.

It was one of few times Elin had actually felt sorry for her, the humiliation and defeat so apparent in the way she cast her watery eyes to the bathroom door, wiping the residual tears from her cheeks. She chewed every bite of food so thoroughly that Elin could feel the lumps getting smaller in her own throat.

NINE

FIRST THING IN THE MORNING Elin's mother was on the phone saying, "What time did you get in? I could use a hand over here with these girls."

Elin hadn't yet dressed. She drew the blanket over her bare legs, and then her waist, and when she moved, her hips were still sore from the drive.

"Late," she lied. "I didn't want to wake you." Her mother's voice, the image of two little sisters, the ridiculous lacy frames on the walls sent Elin into a slow, thick spin. Where was she? Or maybe the question was *when* was she? The sensation was long and sedated, like being pulled through layers of time. Elin drew her knees to her chest like a shield.

"Is she out?" she asked.

"Who?"

"Kate."

"Not yet. I just called."

"I'm not sure what I'm doing here," Elin said. "She's going to leave the hospital in a day or two, pick up her daughters, and act like nothing happened."

Her mother ought to have shot right back, told her she was wrong or in the least *not right*, because that was how they spoke, back and forth like mismatched dancers, one leading, one fumbling, until they switched, and switched again, but here was nothing, a misstep that caused Elin to lean in. "Mom?"

"It's not like we can just hand them back," her mother said. "Not like everything's fine." Her voice cut off, and Elin sat upright.

"What is going on?"

"Well," her mother said. "You've come all this way. . . . I don't exactly know. I don't have any kind of plan. I figured you probably did."

"*Me?*" Elin asked. "Why would I have a plan?"

"Because that's just how you do things."

"And what's that supposed to mean?"

"It's not supposed to mean anything other than what it means."

"Which means what?"

"Oh, good Christ, Elin. I've got to get to work. I've taken all the days off that Roth's could give, and then some. I don't live a fancy lifestyle. These girls will be here with the neighbor if you care to see them."

"Who lives a fancy lifestyle?" Somehow they had fallen straight down the well of conversation that Elin had tried avoiding for years, into the details of her life she'd always withheld because she did not want to hear what her mother had to say about it.

"How would I know?" her mother said. "I've never even been to your house."

"It's not like you don't have my address."

"Like I said, I don't live a fancy lifestyle."

"Is a plane ticket to see me part of some *fancy lifestyle*?"

"Well, if that was the case you might have flown home to see me once or twice."

"Oh, please. I've offered to fly you to Oregon."

"This is not what needs addressing, Elin."

"I realize that—"

The phone rustled around, and then her mother said, "It's in the kitchen cupboard next to the refrigerator. Tell your sister to reach it if you can't."

Then more rustling and Elin felt ashamed, imagining her nieces alone in that house with this strange old woman, their own mother locked away in a psych ward.

"Do they have any idea what's going on?" Elin asked.

"As far as I can tell, no, not the full picture," she said. "I can't bring myself to mention anything close to the truth."

Elin dropped her head in her hand, massaged her temple. "What was Kate doing before this happened?"

"I have no idea."

"You still don't know where she was living or who with?"

"I'm guessing not far from the police station where I picked them up across town. And I assume they were alone. Averlee is the one who called 911."

"And no word from Neal?"

"Ha. No. The only thing the officer said when he called me was, 'There doesn't seem to be a father in the picture.'"

"Why would Kate do this? I can't believe they were right across town this whole time and you never knew."

"That's not for sure. I'm just saying—"

"That's less than ten miles. Isn't it?"

"Ten miles or ten thousand miles, it makes no difference, Elin. She didn't want to be found."

"Those girls are your granddaughters."

"And where the hell have you been?" She didn't give Elin time to answer. "You need to get off your high horse and stop acting like she's just going to show up and everything's going back to the way it was. Stop acting like you're above everybody. I don't need you coming down here trying to blame me for what your sister's done."

"Oh, here we go. Who said I'm blaming you for anything?"

"Don't start. I'm in no mood."

"What are you even talking about?"

"You think you know so much."

"Who said anything about *knowing*?"

"What'd you come here for, Elin? Huh? Why the hell did you agree to come?"

"Why the hell did you *ask* me to come?"

"Goddamnit. I've got to get to work. The girls will be next door if you can bring yourself to lend a hand."

"If I can *bring myself*," Elin said with a snort, but her mother had already dropped off the line.

TEN

THEIR GRANDMOTHER STOOD AT THE side of her truck as if deciding whether or not to leave for work. Averlee, Quincy, and Wink watched from across his yard, Grandma hollering, "They're not allowed in the woods. And don't forget their snack. And call the direct line if you need me. They'll send it straight to the register."

Wink lifted his hand. "We're all right," he said, but their grandmother continued. "If she shows up, stall her. I'm only ten minutes away."

Averlee wondered if this *she* was her mother or Aunt Elin. Could be another relative, too, no telling how many were out there.

"Quincy, use the tissues in your pocket if you need one," their grandmother yelled. "And be good. Both of you."

When the engine started Averlee's chest rumbled, and Quincy covered her ears until their grandmother was out of sight, the truck a dull hum in the distance.

Averlee held Quincy's hand, straining to see Wink's eyes behind his sunglasses, to see if one or the other batted, if that was how he got his name, but the glasses were dark, so dark she wondered if he could see *her*, this strange and tall skinny man in a white T-shirt and tan shorts, his blue boat sneakers, ankles white where his socks should have been.

"You girls know any songs?" he asked.

"Why?" Averlee said.

"To sing."

"Are you a Girl Scout master?" Quincy asked.

Averlee tugged her hand.

"A what?" Wink said.

"Never mind," Averlee said.

"I play the accordion," Wink said. "Not very good, but I thought you might like to sing."

"No, thank you," Averlee said, so politely it sounded rude.

Wink's long shadow stretched the length of Averlee, Quincy, and their shadows combined. He was quiet now, and they were, too, just the sound of her grandmother's white work shirts flapping on the clothesline. A tiny pinwheel spun near Wink's flowerbed and Averlee thought this was why the birdfeeder next to it was empty of birds. Even the scrub jays, like the one at home that ate sunflower seeds from her hand, would be scared of the spinning sparkling blue. Her mother had taught her that.

Wink hooked both thumbs into his front pockets and glanced around at everything except Averlee and Quincy, the way their grandmother had done at the police station, and the ambulance driver, too, before he shut their mother up inside. But now Wink was grinning. He snapped his fingers above his head, and disappeared behind the wooden screen door identical to their grandmother's, the whole house its twin—white and square, and hardly bigger than the slave-worker houses her school had visited at the living museum.

"When's Grandma coming back?" Quincy asked.

"It doesn't matter. Mom'll get here before she does."

"He's weird. What's an accordion?"

"He's nice enough."

Quincy took a tissue from her pocket and wiped her nose, shooting her eyes sideways at Averlee as if doing the thing her grandmother had asked of her was some kind of betrayal.

Averlee picked mosquito bites on her arm, and then the uneven skin around her nails, a habit her mother always hated. She and Quincy were alone in the yard for what felt like a long time and Averlee thought about the snake her grandmother had killed, and then her mother at the kitchen table. She'd gone her whole life seeing nothing like the things she saw these last two days.

She'd never say it, not to anyone, not even Quincy, but there were times when she thought her mother looked ugly, her face puffy in parts, saggy and tired in others, the dark around her eyes making her seem meaner than she was. But when Averlee found her there, sleeping peacefully, her skin was smooth and pretty and white, her hair shiny in the street light from the window, everything about her as untroubled as Averlee had ever seen, and so she'd considered taking the cold medicine to Quincy and going back to bed, even knowing what she knew.

"Let's get out of the sun," Averlee said, but right then Wink returned with a square piece of cardboard in one hand and a gun in the other. Averlee looked again. A gun. A black gun. Quincy dashed behind her.

"An air pistol from the flea market," Wink said.

Averlee felt her eyes grow larger, the glaring sun not enough to draw her lids.

"I'll hang this bull's-eye to the hickory and we'll have us a round."

"We're going to shoot it?" Averlee asked.

"It's just a toy," he said, and Quincy stepped out into view.

Wink pulled a roll of duct tape from his pocket and fastened the cardboard at the top and bottom, running the tape around the tree. The red circles of the target were sloppy but the bull's-eye was round and perfect as if he'd traced a paper cup.

"Ain't nothing to it," Wink said, joining them where they stood, as far back from the target as a couple of cars in a row. He retrieved a handful of black plastic BBs from his other pocket and dropped them into the open slot on the side of the pistol, then snapped it closed. "Just point it like this, aim through the top here, and squeeze back on the trigger." His thin arm seemed unusually long when he held it out, his hand jerking slightly with the suck and pop of the gun.

It wasn't clear he'd hit any part of the target until they got close enough to inspect the tiny pluck in the center of the red. "Don't point it at anybody," Wink said, smiling and offering, handle first, the pistol to Averlee.

ELEVEN

EVERYTHING HAD CHANGED. WHERE PASTURES once sprawled between orange and grapefruit groves, where pockets of pines and swamp and gators had lined the truck routes, miles of anemic concrete roadways had been poured, every corner staked with blue decorative street signs reminiscent of theme parks. Stores Elin had never heard of had fountains out front, cedar and wrought-iron benches to rest on after all the shopping, after walking across half-mile parking lots. Behind all that, matching sand-colored homes spread across the landscape.

Elin was so disoriented by the time she found her mother's driveway that the pang in her chest at seeing her mother's house—the only thing that hadn't changed—defied her relief. The bougainvillea was slightly fatter and lower to the ground, the white siding on the house yellowing with age, the concrete driveway once a canvas for her chalk drawings not nearly as wide or long as she'd remembered, but it reminded her now, as always, of Kate scuffing her rain boots through Elin's chalk drawings the minute Elin looked away.

She forced the brake with her foot, the car already in park, her whole body tensing as if for a fight, but what she felt, looking at her mother's little cracker house, was guilt, and then annoyance at herself for being so short with her on the phone.

Fluke jumped up, paws on the back window, and peered out. Elin followed his line of sight. The neighbor across the yard, an old man, stooped beside a girl with wiry white hair, a smaller version of the same girl who stood to her side.

Elin opened her window, heard a pop, and the girls ran toward a tree, arms in the air, shouting some kind of victory. The older one, Averlee, Elin assumed, was waving a pistol with both hands.

Elin stepped out, immediately light-headed in the blazing sun. She left the engine running, closed the door, and leaned her back into it. Before she could say a word, Averlee was on her, Quincy trotting right behind.

"I know who you are," Averlee said.

"What are you doing with that?" Elin asked.

"It's an air pistol for shooting targets," Averlee said, but Elin was struck mute by the color and shape of her eyes and face, the shape of her fingers, on or off the gun.

"I'm Averlee. This is Quincy."

Fluke barked from inside the car.

"You must be Elin," the man said, offering a hand from nowhere. "My name's Wink Cyrus. I live next door. Just looking after your nieces while Vivvie's at work."

Elin's hand felt lost inside his. "How do you know who I am?" She could have been Kate, after all.

"Your Oregon tag. That's one hell of a drive."

"Oh. Yes. It is. It was. I just came here to . . ." What? Baby-sit? Fight off Kate if she tried taking Averlee and Quincy? ". . . wait here with them today," she said, faltering, her eyes absorbing the girls again, the delicate dip of their noses, sun-blushed cheeks, a line of faint freckles sprinkled across the curves. And all that white curly hair—their father Neal's hair.

But Averlee. What strange fates had overseen Kate and Neal giving birth to a girl who looked exactly like Elin, her hair the only difference, and *that* identical to Neal's, a man Kate eventually claimed to dislike just as much, if not more, than Elin.

"What's your dog's name?" Averlee asked.

Fluke fogged the glass with this breath, his whole body swaying from the strength of a wagging tail. "Fluke. Do you like dogs?"

Averlee didn't answer.

"What about you?" she asked Quincy, who nodded but never quite met her eyes.

"Would you care for a drink?" Wink asked.

"*Oh*. Well . . ." Alcohol could trigger a migraine. But she was sweating and suddenly craving a glass of clear, searing liquid, something icy with a lime.

"I've got lemonade," Wink said.

"Oh. Sure. Thank you."

"We can sit at the picnic table in the shade," Wink said. "I think it's about time for their snack." He went inside his house and Elin felt a sudden pull toward her mother's, the need to crawl inside its walls, draw close the dusty green shutters, have a cookie, take a nap. The house was so much smaller than she remembered, a fraction of the house Elin owned outright with Rudi.

Averlee held up the pistol. "You want to try?"

"Please don't point that at me," Elin said.

"I'm not."

"I bet it hurts to get hit with one of those BBs," Elin said.

Fluke barked again, the sound encapsulated, as if he were far off in the woods. Elin smacked the window to make him stop, and Averlee flinched.

What was taking Wink so long?

Averlee shoved the pistol into Elin's hand. "Just look through the top thing right there and shoot," she said.

"You keep it," Elin said, but it was already in her grip. She joggled it lightly. Across the yard Wink placed a pitcher of lemonade and cups and a plate of cookies on the picnic table. "I'm not sure Fluke and I are staying," Elin said. "Wink seems to have everything under control."

Averlee pulled Quincy by the arm. "Come on," she said. "You need to get out of the sun."

The pistol looked genuine, the black metal barrel, its weight heavier than a toy ought to feel. Elin turned the car off, opened the back door, and Fluke beelined it to the girls, who fell to their knees petting him, laughing, dodging and then jutting their chins toward his tongue. She swung the car door shut and the sun ricocheted off the side mirror, her mother's coffee-can ashtray on the front steps, and even the porch swing behind the wraparound screen.

She slipped free of her sandals and walked barefoot through pockets of hot grey sand in the grass, edging her heels around red ants. Mugginess prickled her arms; her wedding band tightened around the swelling of her finger. She'd thought to remove it, and reconsidered for the sake of conversation with her mother.

"I made you and me some grown-up lemonade," Wink said, handing her a blue glass of icy, lemony liquid. "Grey Goose lemonade."

She sipped, tasted vodka with lemon. "Oh. Hey. Cheers," she said, pleased with the tart burn in her throat. The next thing she knew she was taking aim at the bull's-eye on the tree, Fluke at her feet, Averlee and Quincy leaning in on either side of her. She didn't want to like these girls, her own nieces, a truth that flowed easier with the vodka. They had never been quite *real*. If she'd thought of them, *really* thought of them, they were nothing more than Kate and Neal's offspring, children of a waitress and firefighter, a family made of box-set characters from a story Elin preferred never to hear. But having them on either side of her while such thoughts scurried through her brain made her feel like an ass. Little girls. Nieces. Smelled like honey and sand in the breeze.

Holding a gun made Elin feel foolish, but mostly badly behaved. No sooner had she arrived to look after these kids than a gun was being fired by her own hand. A toy, but it didn't look like one, feel like one, even act like one. Beyond that she knew her mother wouldn't approve, unsure if Kate would either, not to mention Rudi, and it was with everyone in mind that she curled her finger round the trigger and squeezed.

The girls ran to the tree, Fluke at their heels. Averlee shook her head and pointed at the target's outer ring. "Not even close," she said, deadpan.

"Come on back," Elin said.

She tried again, repeatedly, and still couldn't hit any part of the red circle.

"What am I doing wrong?" she asked, but did not want to hear the answer when Wink started to rise.

"No, no," she said. "I got it. Just need some practice, that's all."

By the time she downed her third glass of Grey Goose lemonade, Wink sat broad-legged on his steps, warming up a baby-blue and white pearlized accordion on his lap. He wrested the pleated bellows in and out until the air filled with the sound of wheezing organs. Everything felt oddly harmless, delightfully strange, the pistol now lighter in her hand, less intimidating, the girls holding hands and dancing an impromptu polka at her back.

She fired one BB after another, cocking and squeezing, her pocket heavy with pellets, the pistol cracking off like fireworks until the bull's-eye was finally riddled with holes.

TWELVE

HER MOTHER WOULDN'T BE HOME until close to nine p.m., so Elin had the girls take their baths before she tucked each into the narrow bed, along with assurances that she'd wait until their grandmother returned before leaving. She was still mildly drunk when she wedged her hip onto the bed near their feet to say good night, to say something she thought they ought to hear. But the strain of so much uncertainty bore down on all of them, even Fluke, watching, panting in the center of the floor as if his fur still held the day's heat. Elin was beginning to understand how different Kate's life had been from the one she'd presumed, or rather the one she'd made a point not to think too much about. The kids who'd never been flesh and blood with needs and laughter were not only real-life children, but their faces, especially Averlee's, mirrored Elin's own, and this, more than anything, filled her with an achy sadness. It filled her with worry. How had Kate been living with this? How did she behave toward Averlee? How had *Neal* lived with this? Was seeing Elin every day in the face of his young child too much to bear? Maybe this was why he left. Elin suddenly felt at fault for everything—Kate in the hospital, Neal long gone.

Don't flatter yourself, Elin thought. The world does not revolve around you. Rudi would be the first to say so.

She couldn't take her eyes off her nieces' warm, freshly scrubbed cheeks above the blanket, their lashes long and dark with bath water.

They were blameless children, sisters that her own sister was ready to leave behind.

"Good night," Elin finally said.

"Are you coming again tomorrow?" Averlee asked.

"I suppose so."

"What time?"

"We'll have to see," Elin said.

"You sound like Grandma," Quincy said.

"Do I?"

Neither girl answered, and Elin stood, stepping toward the wall switch.

"My mom said you like secrets," Averlee said.

Elin stopped, a kick in her heart. "What did you say?"

"Nothing."

"What kind of secrets?"

"How should I know? They're secrets."

"Why would she tell you that?"

Averlee shrugged.

"What else did she say?"

"Nothing."

"Is that right." Elin braced the doorframe. "Hmn," she said, making every attempt at playing cool. "That's funny. A joke, I guess. What was she talking about when she said this?"

"I don't remember."

"Try."

Averlee clamped her jaw shut and squeezed the edge of the blanket at her throat.

"You're not in trouble," Elin said. "I'm just curious what she meant."

"How long are we going to be here?" Quincy asked.

"We'll know more tomorrow. Not long, I don't think."

"Will we have to move?" Averlee asked.

"Have you moved a lot?"

"I guess not."

"I don't see why you would," Elin said. "Listen, about the secrets . . . if there's something you promised not to tell, it's okay to tell me."

"Why?"

"Because. Maybe your mom was right. Maybe I *do* like secrets, which means I'm good at keeping them. You have any you'd like to share?"

Averlee shook her head.

"What about you, Quincy?" Elin asked.

She shook her head, too.

Elin stared as if a deeper concentration might reveal if they were telling the truth.

"Promise we'll see you again?" Averlee asked.

"Of course you'll see me again. But right now it's late, and so sweet dreams, and all that," she said, and hit the switch. An automatic nightlight glimmered near the floor.

"Good night," their voices harmonized in the murky orange glow.

Back in the living room, Elin sat on the sofa with Fluke, gently tugging his ears down his head, his eyes bobbing into sleep. She glanced at her phone. No new messages.

Why would Kate have said such a thing about her? Why did she insist on reminding Elin of the past? It had been years, decades, since Elin had given thought to that night when she was younger than her nieces were now, asleep in the very same room. Voices rumbling down the hall, her parents, she'd thought, but then a stranger's voice rose above the others. She'd crawled out of bed and peeked around the corner to see her mother crying into her hands on the sofa. Three policemen had pulled kitchen chairs up around her. "Looks like we have a visitor," one said, and her mother jumped. "Oh, Elin. Sweetheart. You need to go back to bed."

71

"Why are they here?" Elin asked, her calves chilled from the open front door, standing as she was in a thin nightgown, and thinking of the cold hose her mother had used on their speckled hound's face and ears that morning, blood running off into the sandy patches of grass beneath the bathroom window where, inside, Elin had heard a noise. She'd stood on the edge of the tub, balanced above the bathwater, peering out.

"We can talk about all of this tomorrow," her mother said. "Let me tuck you back in."

"Where's Dad? I want *him* to tuck me in."

Elin now bolted into standing at the sound of her mother's key in the door. Fluke barked, leaped off the sofa.

"Stay," Elin said, as sternly as she'd ever spoken the word. Fluke froze.

"Will you look at this?" Her mother suddenly there, dropping her purse onto the table, holding her arms out to Elin. "And her little dog Toto, too."

"Mom."

Then holding her, squeezing in a way she'd rarely done, and Elin hugging her back.

"Are they asleep?" her mother asked, and then held Elin at arm's length, looking her over with puckered eyes, aged ten more years. Elin touched the corner of her own eye, the thin lines her mother hadn't yet seen.

"Who?" Elin asked.

"*Who*? The lizards in the bush. What do you mean, who? Averlee and Quincy."

"Sorry. I'm tired. Yes. As far as I know, they're asleep."

"What's his name?" Her mother looked down. Fluke worried his sights between Elin and her mother.

"Fluke."

Her mother laughed. "What kind of name is that?"

Before Elin could answer, her mother brought a hand to Elin's shoulder, a single pat, like a slap. "Fluke," she said, and then walked to the kitchen and poured a glass of milk, her choice of evening drink as far back as Elin could remember. "Would you like some?"

"No. Thank you."

"You look good," she said, her back still turned. "Healthy. Happy. Life out there must be agreeing with you."

Clearly Rudi hadn't called looking for her. Elin would have heard a trace of it in her mother's voice. "Thanks," Elin said. "I guess so."

Her mother faced her, glass in hand. "So, what'd you and the girls do all day?"

"Oh, we just. You know. Not much. Played around. Wink seems nice. The girls are . . . interesting."

"Spooky how much Averlee looks like you," her mother said.

"I'm sure it pleases Kate to no end."

Her mother swallowed her milk, a touch of mania about her, as if her eight-hour shift was still buzzing beneath her skin.

"Why would Kate do this?" Elin asked. "She cut off all contact with us. If she was living alone with the girls then who did she think would take them? I assume the only reason we even found out what happened is because the police located her next of kin."

"She called you, though," her mother said. "The night before."

"I know. But it's not like she made a lot of sense. Going on about the time she nearly drowned. I guess it was some kind of warning. I don't know. She sounded drunk."

"What do you think we ought to do?" her mother said.

"About what?"

"These girls. And God knows what else. She won't even let us in there to talk to her, to see what the hell is going on. I'll tell you this much, she looked bad. She looked awful. The nurse *knew* her, too, said Kate had been in before."

"For the *same thing*?"

"She wouldn't tell me."

Elin tossed her hands above her head. "This is ridiculous."

"I don't imagine the law's going to hand those girls back over to Kate. That officer left a message on my cell earlier, but I didn't get it until after my shift. Maybe that's what it was about. He just said to call him. I tried on my way home, but he was already gone and no one at the station would tell me what it was he wanted."

"Well, I'm pretty sure it's against the law to try and kill yourself," Elin said.

Her mother turned and rinsed her glass at the sink.

Elin gathered her purse and sandals and moved toward the door. She pointed Fluke in the same direction and he sat beneath the doorknob, watching her, watching her mother, his eyebrows flickering in distress. "The girls need some new clothes," Elin said. "I'll come back first thing in the morning and take them shopping." She imagined them wide-awake, listening to everything she said. She rummaged through her purse for her keys. Fluke scooted out of the way as she opened the door.

"Did you say anything to them about Kate?" her mother said.

"What on earth would I say?"

"Did they ask about her?"

"No."

Her mother gripped the edge of the counter behind her hips. "It's been a long time," she said. "It isn't easy, dealing with . . ." She gestured to the living room as if all their troubles had gathered there. "I'm not even sure what to call what's happened."

"Have you really not seen Neal since before Kate disappeared?" Elin asked, the vodka thicker in her head than she'd realized, but even so, with the question now posed, it was clear as any thought she'd ever had that she'd been wanting to ask it for days.

Her mother crossed her arms. "Last I heard he was living in Arizona."

"*Arizona?* What's he doing out there?"

"Your guess is as good as mine."

"Who told you that?"

"His cousin Angelina when I saw her at Roth's years ago. She didn't know exactly where. Arizona was all."

"Do you think we should try to find him? I mean, he *is* their father whether we like it or not."

"I *did* try to find him. I started looking right after Kate disappeared. I thought she might have taken off to wherever he was."

"Did she?"

"I don't know. I never found either one. I tried searching the computer, still do, but nothing ever shows up. I can't even find Angelina on there."

"Arizona," Elin said.

"I'd die a happy woman if I never laid eyes on him again. I can't imagine otherwise for you."

Elin squeezed the keys in her fist. This was the mother she liked. The one who hated Neal. The one who'd thrown an orange tear-shaped lamp across the room at his head. "He actually came to say good-bye," her mother told her years ago. "Can you believe that? *Good-bye?* I told him he had no business getting together with Kate in the first place, and you know what he said? He said, 'What about your granddaughters?' So I threw a lamp at him."

"Oh my God, Mom, you didn't."

"I did. And the son of a bitch ducked and came up laughing."

Elin glanced into the living room at the orange lamp on the end table, the white, modern-styled one on the other.

"I guess I better hit the road," Elin said. "The place I'm staying is a ways out of town."

"I didn't mean to get so mad at you on the phone this morning. I appreciate you coming all this way."

Elin couldn't recall her mother ever apologizing for anything, and she took a step back, curled her fingers around the doorknob. "It's okay. I needed a break," she said, the humidity still hanging on, working its way through the screened porch, globbing onto her skin, while her mind continued with a mind of its own, peeling back unpleasant pieces of memory. "Working a lot, and all that. I'll see you in the morning," she said, and was careful, as she'd been taught, not to let the screen slam shut behind her.

THIRTEEN

WHENEVER ELIN HAD TROUBLE SLEEPING she thought of snow. Not only here, in the rose-colored bedroom with its lacy-framed portraits, but at home, in the *Ehebett* with the steady white noise of Rudi's breath in her ear. It wasn't just any snow she thought of, it was her first, like a love, like an initiation she'd stumbled through, dazedly ecstatic. Mount Hood, not long after she arrived in Oregon, her ears popping as the VW climbed the switchback, and then the first white patch tucked between a hollow in the distant hills. "There it is," she said, and shut the radio off as if to honor, to witness the way she'd been delivered by magic into the tallest pines and peaks in the universe, to a place where it snowed. No more than a minute later, thick, cottony flakes hovered toward the windshield. "So *gently,*" she said, surprised at the delicate dance, but that was right before the onslaught of crystals blinded out all and sundry and made her squeal. She was alone, not just in the car, but in the world, frightened and euphoric with possibility, and this made her laugh, surrounded by a white so bright it felt holy. A clarified beauty, *virtuous*, she thought, and drove on in this way for the better part of thirty minutes until the sun broke through at the top of the mountain and varnished the snow with a blinding glare, forcing Elin to park in the first space near the stone lodge. She closed her eyes and wept against the steering wheel. "What is *this*?" she said. But she knew. Too much happiness was what it was. "Too much," she said, after a lifetime of arrears.

On her way down the mountain she'd stopped at the first pay-phone and called Neal. Snow flew sideways past the glass and she remembered Neal telling her about the first time he saw the air fill with white ash after a warehouse fire, the way it had floated, eerily, with the slow beauty of snow, and how guilty he'd felt for being taken by it, how alluring it was in the wake of devastation.

It only took a second to understand the call would not go the way she'd imagined. Nothing would. And that was one thing, that was run-of-the-mill heartbreak, love won and lost between them, but the rest drew on a vision that was never meant to be seen.

"I'm seeing someone," he said.

A minute later she was back in her car, a cold key in a cold ignition. She leaned over the gearshift and hollered as if down a well. "Fuck all y'all!" she yelled, and the snow gathered like virgin wool all around her. *Like virgin wool*, she wanted to say, wanted to scream into the phone that would have already turned her fog of warm breath into a white layer of frost on the mouthpiece. But what did she expect? She had left him, disappeared in the face of explaining all that she could not say.

Now snow was miles and months from even a *possibility*, and the B and B's smell of warm, polished cedar panes filled Elin with a chilly, cramping sorrow. She tossed off the comforter and jimmied the window up as if in defiance of her own needs, searching instead for the opposite of what she wanted: a warm breeze. But the atmosphere at sea level in the tropics—three o'clock in the morning be damned—hung thickly, the scent of grass and magnolias stuck outside. Only the pulse of cicadas pierced the screen—*click-buzzzzzz, click-buzzzzz*—a chorus of broken sprinklers. Males, she knew, from her book on insects, puffed and yearning for mates, and against her will she thought of Rudi's smile in the moonlight last week—his lips, and then the way she'd reached over without thinking while he talked and talked, and slid that small flip of hair across his forehead.

She gasped and jerked her hand from the window, singed by the realization that the little sprig of cowlick in Rudi's hairline that she'd always been so fond of was identical to her father's, right down to the tiny widow's peak made up of several stray hairs.

She shoved the sticky window down, flung herself onto the bed, and covered her face with the sheet. She would force herself to sleep, to forget, to dream of snow. But the ceiling fan whined like a donkey braying off in a field, and Fluke's body was hot at her feet.

She sat up. A total of twenty-five messages on her phone. She switched on the speaker mode and held it out as if watching a video. "Where are you?" Rudi said, his voice cutting the dark. Fluke opened his eyes.

Elin showed him the glowing phone as if he'd understand and in fact he seemed to, drifting back to sleep, even as she played the beginning of each message, unable to bear the digressions toward each end.

"Elin. Just answer your phone."

"Elin. Please."

"*Please.*"

"Elin. Look."

"Elin. It's not as if you aren't aware . . ."

"This is crazy."

"Two days, Elin."

"I'm begging you."

"Elin, listen to me, I'm considering calling the police."

"*Ach, du Scheisse!*"

"Four days is a long time to disappear."

"All right, Elin, at least grant me this one thing."

The next message began with dead air, then sniveling. Throat clearing, nose wiping, utterances that made no sense. And then, "I'm sorry," he said, as clear as if he'd crawled across the sheets and whispered through her hair.

Morning arrived with Elin transfixed on the edge of her bed, head aching, not a migraine, but eyes inflamed from staring too long in the dark. She wrapped her arms around herself, thinking of that flip of her father's hair, Rudi's hair—what she wouldn't give for a pair of scissors and one more night in the *Ehebett*. But she would force herself to forget. Getting rid of her past had been her strong suit, a mindful hobby for which she had a knack, going all the way back to those early years, kids asking Elin and Kate what it was like growing up without a dad. "What's it like to walk on two feet?" Elin would say. It's no kind of question to ask without something to compare it to, some stark before-and-after frame of reference. What had always been so thin, it seemed, were her memories of ever having had a father in the first place. Elin was six when he died, Kate five, and Elin's surest memory was so small she wasn't convinced it actually belonged to her or if she'd borrowed it from a story or a dream. Barely tall enough to see outside, and even then it felt as if she were on her tiptoes, peering out a window in the upper part of the wooden back door. In the yard her father swung Kate by her wrists, her dark hair flailing, their laughter loud enough to penetrate the glass. But then her father faltered and nearly toppled into the grass. Kate stumbled, still laughing, while her father clutched his knees and hunched, bracing, as if catching his breath. Her mother appeared from the side of the house, her stride long and hard, direct in the way she came at Elin and Kate when they'd done something wrong. A camera swung around her neck and she grabbed it steady. Kate seemed oblivious to whatever was happening, dropping herself into a line of cartwheels in the opposite direction while her father stood upright, brushed his cowlick to the side, and grasped her mother's arm. His stance was tall and serious as he spoke directly into her face as if making sure the words were not only heard but *seen*—he was just that close. Her mother shot back, pointing a finger in his face, her mouth a tight slit of quiet, spitting words Elin couldn't hear. Kate's hands froze in the air, then dropped to her sides as she approached, lacing her fingers through her mother's, and then her father's, while behind the closed door Elin's insides warmed, the tips of her fingers sweating on the wooden trim. Her breath made an icy fog on the window, and when she wiped it away, the yard, even the space between the trees, wobbled with a mystifying heartache Elin would forever link to autumn sun.

FOURTEEN

"WELL, THAT'S JUST AWFUL," SHUG said, sliding the silver pitcher of syrup toward Elin, who quickly poured more than she needed, her waffle floating in a maple pool on the blue and white Wedgewood china. She wasn't sure why she'd told Shug about Kate being in the hospital. Divulging something so personal to a stranger was tacky at best, but that wasn't the problem. The person foremost on Elin's mind right now was Rudi. She was starting to remember him with tenderness, with a tinge of guilt she didn't understand. She didn't want to understand. She was angry. She thought she was. And in the right, no doubt about it, which was where she planned to remain. All this venting about her irresponsible, yet obviously *ill*, sister felt like a lie, even as Elin let go the truest details.

"It *is* awful," Elin said, speaking of one thing, meaning another, her mind incapable of suppressing Rudi's apology, the final confirmation that what Lotus had told her was true, his apology as good as a photograph of his dick in Poppy's mouth.

She took a bite, set her fork aside, and drew a long breath through her nose, chewing quickly as heat rose beneath her skin. She swallowed in stages, and after a long gulp of well water she said, "But that's my sister," as if she had nothing but disdain for a woman who, in the midst of some awful misery, had tried to kill herself. The room went silent, only Fluke chomping a bone at her feet. Elin was heartless, a part of her was, and she sat with that, aware of her capacity to shift half her attention toward the sun warming the wooden shelves, the rows of antique books—Twain, Faulkner, O'Connor, Chekhov, Tolstoy, Dostoyevsky—their dusty paper scent in the air.

"Well," Shug said. "If there are things you need to work out with your family . . ."

"Oh, I don't—"

"It's been slow around here. You're welcome to stay as long as you like. I'm happy to discount your room."

It's not as if you aren't aware, Rudi had started to say. He might have ended with any number of things. Awareness bloomed like algae in Elin's chest. I've done nothing, she thought. *My mom says you like secrets.*

"That's kind of you," Elin said, unsure if she'd followed the thread of their conversation correctly. "I need to figure out a way. To help her." Maybe she should leave. Not just the B and B, but Florida altogether. She could have taken a vacation anywhere in the world. She could have thrown Rudi out of the house. Why *had* she come *here*? For *Kate*? Elin nearly laughed. Her mother had been right to ask.

"I appreciate your offer." Elin stood, took a step toward the foyer. "And allowing Fluke to hang around with you while I'm gone this morning. I should have kenneled him. I don't know what I was thinking."

"It doesn't sound to me like there was much time for thinking."

"I suppose."

"He's a comfort, I imagine. Probably best that he came with you. I don't mind for a minute. I appreciate the company."

"I have a feeling things will turn around within a couple of days. I'm afraid I need to get going. My nieces—"

"Oh, those poor girls. Go, go, go," Shug said, coming to her feet, shooing with one hand, clearing plates with the other, and for a second Elin caught a glimpse of what it might feel like to live alone in this handsome house, preferring the company of a dog, of strangers whose problems departed with them, leaving behind idle rooms and afternoons to pull a book from a shelf, take to a corner chair where nothing else would be expected for the day. The idea of such solitude exhilarated the tiny hairs on Elin's arms.

"Thank you," she said.

Shug barely had a chance to reply before Elin escaped out the front door through the shady blanket of willow limbs drooping in the sun.

FIFTEEN

MONTHS BEFORE JACKSON DIED HE had sat in an aluminum-framed lawn chair holding hands with Vivvie standing at his side. They faced a pile of chopped pinewood at the edge of the backyard, above them the most transparent night sky Vivvie had ever seen, glittering with stars. Lightning bugs, like buoyant embers, sparked the distant dark. Jackson let go of Vivvie's hand and attempted to strike a match in his lap but snapped several sticks in half before handing the matchbox to her. She lit one on the first try. The girls had been asleep in the house for hours. They would wake in the morning to a circle of ash in a yard that was their playground, wake to some kind of summer campfire that mysteriously had not included them. It would be the first of too many things never to be explained, and the thought seared Vivvie's already fragile heart. She held the burning match, stalled by the question: What do you love more, Vivien Fenton, your *love* for Jackson, or *Jackson*? She tossed the match onto the woodpile. A whoosh of yellow, tinged in ruby red, ignited the air.

The chorus of crickets gave way to the crackle of bark, cut grass to lighter fluid, and finally scorched tar.

"I can't argue," Jackson said. He didn't touch her, glanced only at the box of photographs near Vivvie's feet. "I've got no right to begrudge you as to what goes on after."

He was referring to a conversation they'd begun earlier that day. Vivvie had woken with a purpose, her head on the pillow, face toward the wall, and had said, "Sometimes it's better to let the very best of us go up in flames." She'd avoided his eyes throughout the day, and then, after the girls were in bed, she dragged the box of photographs across the length of the yard to the pit of logs in the sandy soil. "I don't want to remember," she said. "I already can't stand having them in the house."

"All right," he said. "All right." His fingers loosened, and the first photograph, a black and white taken on the Carrabelle River before they were married, began to fall. How young they appeared, Vivvie's long hair tied with a kerchief that Jackson had freed with a hook of his finger, and beneath them the wool blanket on the shore, orange and green and sun-scented with animal fleece, with sex, and their cheeks sheer with affection fanning out past the edges of the photograph—all of it fluttering into the fire, coiling against the heat.

"Burnt offerings," Jackson said, meant as a joke, meant to appease her, tracing around a guilt she knew he carried for a world over which he had no control. Maybe he went along with it because he thought it would push her toward a new life more quickly, make it easy for her to find someone new. "You're still young, Viv," he'd told her months before. "So beautiful and strong, and so damn fun to be around." Maybe saying that made him feel valiant, selfless. He was wrong about everything.

Vivvie took his hand, feeling tiny sleeping faces at her back, envisioning what their eyes would never see, all that their minds and hearts would never know. She let go and clutched a hefty, clumsy stack of photos, chucked it onto the pyre. They scattered between logs and caught quickly, emitting sparks and blue flames, a plastic chemical smell that made her sick.

SIXTEEN

THE MORNING HUMIDITY CAUSED A spongy feeling on the back of Vivvie's neck, wisps of hair slipping free of the hairclip loosened by sweat. She hadn't slept well. Summer had never felt this hot. She was born and raised here, and no one could tell her different.

But the girls had wanted to wait outside for Elin so Vivvie busied herself nearby, deadheading petunias and brushing aside grass clippings from the sidewalk after Wink's early morning mow. Wink sat on his steps, whittling a stick with a silver pocketknife that caught the sun. After a quick hello, Vivvie avoided his attention. She'd been taken over by an unexpected shyness she didn't understand.

Twenty minutes later, she happened to look up. Wink waved his pocketknife, more at the girls than her, it seemed, and Averlee and Quincy smiled and lifted opposite hands, like a two-headed girl in a dance. Vivvie marveled at their ability to sit so close for so long in this heat without bickering.

Wink waved again, this time at Vivvie. In all the years they'd been neighbors, Vivvie had never seen him whittle, and here paper-thin strips of blond wood gathered at his bare feet, his lips pursed in concentration. Not long ago he'd come through her line at Roth's, handed her a twenty, and said, "I've known you, what . . . a decade? And other than the fact that you seem awfully fond of that jasmine at the side of your house the way you linger on watering it every morning, you're kind of a *mystery*, Vivvie Fenton."

She'd felt herself go red and immediately looked to see who might have heard. But heads were turned, women comparing prices, tapping melons, the world carrying on even as it shifted to one side. Wink grinned, waiting for her smart-aleck reply. This was how they knew one another—a baiting banter volleying back and forth—and a sentence from all those spy films did in fact form in Vivvie's mind: *I could tell you but then I'd have to kill you.* Vivvie's mouth clamped shut and her eyes saw nothing but the tattered bill in her hand, her thoughts knotted, incapable of whistling past the image of him watching her through his window.

She gestured a hand to Wink across the yard, smiling weakly beneath the dawning realization that her granddaughters were the cause of the shyness. Mercy me. Small voices and peanut butter breath. Fingerprints on the plate glass window. These little sisters had laid Vivvie bare. A ragged skin peeled back, a blaze of light shining on the person she used to be.

SEVENTEEN

ELIN'S NIECES WERE WAITING ON the steps when she pulled into the driveway, knees tucked together like a set of dolls positioned so as not to fall forward. The humidity had kinked their hair even farther above their heads, and when Elin made eye contact through the windshield they gazed like feral cats she had the urge to cradle, but mostly feared.

She got out and stepped back as if from the strange thoughts she was having. "See? I came just like I promised," she said, hearing an unintended sarcasm in her voice. It was already hot and getting hotter. "Shit," she murmured, fanning her shirt.

"Where you girls headed this morning?" Wink called out, shaving a small piece of wood with what appeared to be a pocketknife.

"Shopping for new clothes," she said.

"That ought to give me enough time," he said, and went back to the stick in his hands.

Before Elin had a chance to ask what he meant, her mother opened her screen door but hung back, her hand on the trim, looking older than Elin had noticed the night before, the dark patches now visible in the sunlight. She squeezed a red dishtowel in a fist at her side.

This house, her mother, the whole damn state was like a box of Cracker Jacks, strange memories the cheap prize at the bottom. Here was Kate ripping an Etch A Sketch from Elin's fingers at the kitchen table. Instead of yanking it back, Elin had screamed loudly, fiercely, as if Kate had taken an ax to her, her breath nearly spent when their mother lunged and swung at them with a dish towel, stinging their cheeks and ears, swatting and batting as if they were a swarm of bees. And then her mother snatched the Etch A Sketch from the table and slammed it to the floor. Shards of red and silver plastic ricocheted and stung Elin's ankles beneath the table. Elin kept her head bowed, unable to suppress a grin. She cupped her face as if crying, but it was laughter she hid in her hands, uncontrollable laughter. Let Kate try and use it now, she thought.

Home.

Her mother had been eyeing Elin's car since sticking her head out the door—hood, grille, headlights, tires. With the sun-bleached truck in front, and the tin-roofed, century-old cracker house to the side, Elin's Audi was as showy as a float in a parade, a metallic grey rocket ship sent from the future. "If you're going to have the girls out in the sun you might want to pick up some sunscreen," her mother said. "I'm all out."

Had she even greeted her? "Good morning, Mom," Elin said.

"Good morning." Her mother surprised her with a half smile.

"Come on," Averlee said, taking Quincy by the hand as she stood. "Let's get this show on the road."

Elin grinned to herself.

"Reminds me of someone," her mother said.

Elin's stomach roiled as she opened the rear door. "Scoot on in there and put your belts on," she said.

"I know how to do it," Averlee said, guiding Quincy in first.

Her mother *tsked* at Elin's back. "The boss," she said.

Elin fanned her shirt again. "I assume you mean me," she said over her shoulder.

"If it walks like a duck, quacks like a duck . . ."

"Any news about my sister?"

Averlee's head shot up from the backseat. If thoughts could fly, hers would have launched like birds through the window.

Her mother peered in Wink's direction, wiped her hairline on her arm, and didn't meet Elin's eyes when she said, "I'm getting ready to call over there." She surveyed the car again. "I just tried that officer who left the message last night. He wasn't in yet."

Elin nodded at the ground, the trees, and now she too couldn't take her eyes from the car, as if it were the thing at the center of this tale—a vessel, a magic carpet, a gift from Rudi's fairytale life, delivering Elin into this most unlikely land.

EIGHTEEN

THE TREE-LINED STREET, SIDEWALK CAFÉS, and coffee shops of Winter Park reminded Elin of Portland with a grander, European flair. But such consolation was no match for the overriding fact that she was still in Florida, no more than five miles from where she grew up, as if the last decade of her life had been nothing more than a dream of a grown-up life out west, only to wake and find herself in Florida, two kids in the backseat, and married to Neal.

She glanced behind her. The girls had leaned into their windows, gaping at the colorful shops.

"*This* is where we're buying clothes?" Averlee asked.

Elin searched for a parking space. "Why am I not surprised that your mother has never brought you here?" she said as much to herself as to them, and directed the air conditioning toward her face in anticipation of getting out of the car and into the heat. She sucked at the chill as if it were oxygen meant to clear her head. She joggled her temple. Was mentioning Kate something she was supposed to do? Or so obviously *not* what she was supposed to do? She bore her finger between the thready muscles. No headache. Not yet.

A turn signal flickered down the block as a car wedged out of a space, inches at a time. Elin flipped her blinker and waited, checked the side mirror for traffic behind her, and was startled by the reflection of a man with light, wavy hair and black sunglasses. He was singing, or at least mouthing the words, tapping a finger on the steering wheel, and bobbing his head. She glanced up at the rearview mirror for a fuller picture. "For fuck's sake," she whispered. The universe had one hell of a sense of humor. The man was driving a canary-colored Karmann Ghia with the canvas top rolled down. She'd thought of Neal only seconds before and here was the car he used to drive when she lived with him. Same color, same make, if she wasn't mistaken.

Elin rolled her window down, stuck her arm out, and motioned for him to go around. He finally hiked his shoulders, mouthed a sheepish "oh," laughed, and made a move, lifting a hand to wave as he passed. At least it wasn't Neal.

They had to walk five blocks before finding a children's clothing store. The Pretty Penny, located on Winter Park's exclusive Park Avenue.

"What's that smell?" Quincy said as the three of them stepped inside.

"Vanilla bubblegum, I think," Elin said.

"I don't like it," Quincy said, in the exact moment a saleswoman—too young to be draped in pearls—approached them by way of small, high-heeled steps across the pastel-blue carpet.

"Me neither," Elin said.

"Can I help you find something?" The woman's accent had a tinge of Florida sorority.

"No," Elin said. "They're. We're—"

"She's our aunt," Averlee cut in.

Elin covered her own grin. "Just putting that out there," she said, "just in case." But the young woman didn't seem to have a sense of humor. Elin glanced uncomfortably at the miniature outfits on the wall—green aprons complete with tiny tools in the pockets. Kitchen aprons with frills, a little too French in Elin's view, a little too grown up, and next to those hung vest-pocket suits for boys. For playing dress-up? For every day? Elin blinked repeatedly, not really wanting to understand.

The saleswoman shifted her hip and slowly ground her high heel into the carpet, a nervous-looking habit, perhaps to fill the void. "Well. Okay," she said. "I'm Tiff if you need anything," and off she went in her tiny steps to the counter, hands on hips before dropping them, forcefully, and adjusting her hair with a sigh that sounded a lot like frustration.

"Go ahead and look around, pick out a few things," Elin said. It occurred to her that she'd gone through all of the cash in her wallet on the way to Florida, and now her debit card was about to show a purchase, which Rudi could view online within seconds, no doubt gleaning all kinds of satisfaction from finally knowing where she was. And that where she was was *here*, in *Florida*, and on top of every-thing, buying *kids'* clothes for her nieces, because, who else? Oh, she had reconnected with her family! Wasn't that exactly what she'd needed? Wasn't that exactly what he'd been trying to get her to do for years?

The girls circled the tables like sluggish fish, eyes shimmering re-flections of jazzy fabrics and sunlight streaming through the windows. They appeared to have gone into shock.

"For the love of God," Elin said, and plucked T-shirts and shorts from a nearby stack. "What size do you wear?" she asked, holding a shirt in front of Quincy, who stiffened at Elin's proximity. Elin reared back and tried to compose herself. "Let's get this show on the road," she said, and scooped up a pile of possibilities, including belts and underwear, and handed everything to Averlee. "Take these into a dressing room and try them on."

"Whatever you say, Captain."

This was why Elin never wanted children. Mercurial little crea-tures capable of doing or saying anything at anytime, getting away with unreasonable acts, wild beings uninhabited by rationale. She should know, she'd been one herself. Kate, too, and even more so. You could not train a child like a dog, and while Elin was well aware of how awful that might sound if spoken out loud, she also clung wholeheartedly to its truth.

"I'll wait here," Elin said, and by the time she sat in the floral wing-back chair across from the dressing room stalls, the latch on the door had already clicked in place. She checked her phone. Nothing new from Rudi. Nothing from her mother, and in the absence of some kind of word about Kate, Elin's irritation at her sister's lame cry for help, or attention grabbing, or whatever it was she was trying to prove, had *always* been trying to prove, rose to a new level. Kate was the first to scream in an argument, first to stomp and curl a fist, first to leap to the worst possible conclusion. It was as if she believed the world was designed to slight her and she had no choice but to lunge and sucker punch a kidney in order to seize what she considered hers.

As for the rare times when she wasn't being confrontational? She was lying low, scheming her next move, like the time Elin found herself vulnerable after two glasses of wine and confessed to Kate how suffocated she felt by having only ever lived within miles of where they grew up. She revealed her fantasies of walking out the door and never looking back, and she asked Kate if she too had to suppress the urge to get away, to crawl out from under a constant, invisible weight. And what had Kate so breezily replied? "Not really. But that doesn't mean you don't deserve a decent life, Elin. You should just go for it and see what Neal does. I wouldn't be surprised if he follows you. Of course he'll follow you. We should all be so lucky to have someone look at us the way he looks at you." How had Elin not realized that the bright tone in Kate's voice wasn't sincerity but rather Kate's own excitement for a future about to unfold? It shocked Elin still, how quickly she'd been willing to believe her, how moved she'd been by the simple gesture. She hung onto Kate's words like a lucky talisman dangling from the rearview mirror on the day she drove away.

Fuck her. If Kate had really wanted to kill herself she could have used a surefire method. Slit her wrists or something.

Elin covered her eyes, on a roll it seemed, toward epic levels of uncharitable, disgusting convictions. She dropped her hand in her lap. Then again. How dare Kate put everyone through this, put her *own daughters* through this, and then *refuse visitors*? What would she do if Elin just showed up in the flesh? Have security throw her out?

Elin rubbed her eyes, drawing the ache to the surface.

If the girls were talking she couldn't hear. Just the faint rustling and buckling of clothes, white noise making her drowsier than she'd already suddenly become.

When the latch finally slid free it was Averlee who appeared. Elin would have bet money on Quincy coming out first, Averlee showing her off like a prized goat. But here was Averlee in an outfit of eerie resemblance to Elin's—a cobalt blue T-shirt and tan capris.

Averlee stood before the tall mirror in the open room and gazed at herself as if she were alone. She appeared smaller, sweeter, more delicate in reflection.

"I can't get this belt," Quincy called from inside the stall.

Elin stood behind Averlee, the wall at their backs covered in a red and black tapestry depicting folktales—wolves, tall pines, cabins with smoky chimneys, birds in flight. Above them a skylight shined a cone of yellow sun onto their heads. It was as if they stood on stage, two identical selves gazing forward with rounded eyes, their mouths hoop-shaped discs like a couple of stunned Russian dolls no longer stacked, no longer hidden one inside the other.

"Averlee?" Quincy called again.

Averlee sighed deeply at herself. "My mom will never see me in this, will she?"

What a morbid thing to say. She might look like Elin but she was definitely her mother's daughter. Of all the replies that came to Elin's mind (*Why would you say that, it isn't true, of course she will*) followed by an imaginary round of enthusiastic laughter meant to clobber the mawkishness into submission and declare it a joke—nothing, not a single utterance, managed to fizzle past Elin's lips. She was struck numb. And now too many beats were passing in anticipation that something should be said, the right words refusing to save her, save them both, and the next thing Elin knew she was touching Averlee's hair, petting its length through her fingers, a downy silk, gossamer threads just like her father's, spun so light they felt like nothing at all.

"I don't know how to do this belt," Quincy whined.

Elin held the velvety strands in both hands, forgetting she was really just a stranger to this child. Her old desire to barrel smack-dab through the middle of things as if what was happening had no effect, as if nothing had *ever* happened, was no match for this small face in the mirror, her words as true as any Elin would ever hear. Kate was going to succeed, one way or another. She was going to leave these children behind. Elin saw her swallowing pills in the dark, heard the sound of her voice threatening a razor behind the bathroom door, felt the white hot sting of Kate's heel striking Elin's jaw beneath the ocean, the spongy give of Kate's breastbone on the shore as Elin forced the life back inside her.

She released Averlee's hair, stepped aside, and rested her fingertips against her own lips, recalling how lifeless her sister's had felt against them, the funneling fire in her own chest, a cauterized burn from exhaling more fiercely than seemed humanly possible for an eleven-year-old girl.

My mother said you like secrets.

Elin touched Averlee's shoulder, spun her around, and kneeled until their faces were inches apart. "Don't be angry at her," she said, feeling a flash behind one eye, and now another as she stared into what appeared to be her own eyes freakishly reflecting back.

She stood just long enough to reach the armrest and sit in the chair.

"I got it," Quincy said, standing before them, her outfit slovenly mismatched, red stripes and yellow dots, a tiny clown with wild hair, smiling and happy for all the world to see.

NINETEEN

"THERE HAVE BEEN CALLS TO Children's Services," Officer Moore told Vivvie on the phone. "From your daughter's neighbor, about her not looking after her kids. You understand she's sick. Not the suicide attempt. That's not the sick I'm referring to here."

"I don't know what you mean," Vivvie said, but that was a lie, wasn't it? Hadn't she understood the moment she saw Kate's scraggy arms and legs, that tremor in her hand? And yet she'd pretended with the nurse and doctor, pretended with Elin and the girls, pretended with her own mind that what had flowed through Jackson's veins could not possibly be flowing through her daughter's. Kate, a young, galloping surge wherever she went, the way she'd thumped and jumped through the house, into the truck, across the yard and up a tree, as if to feel her own body, as if in defiance of her own future, a destiny that had her pinned to a bed. Maybe all that anger was a way of igniting herself, her spiteful poetry nothing more than a premonition, an awareness that life, from the start, had been stacked against her.

"I'm not supposed to give advice," Officer Moore said. "But if I were you, I'd get to the courts before something happens. I apologize for being so blunt, but having to untangle the legal system along with everything else—"

"Why would the hospital tell you this and not me?" she asked, unable to stop herself from dodging, from giving voice to one injustice as if it might somehow alleviate the other.

"The past complaints included that she was sick. It's part of my report, Mrs. Fenton. And that report is public."

An hour later Vivvie was still stuck at the kitchen table, feeling the emptiness of the rooms around her, each grounded by neglect for so long, nothing touched or moved, even her eyes not fully taking in what was before her throughout decades-long comings and goings, her dull, meek routine as predictable and pathetic as a widow's worn path to a grave.

Having her granddaughters here, their eyes roaming her house, Averlee's particularly intent, as if searching for the thing she was sure was hidden there, returned Vivvie to the terror she had felt over losing her daughters after losing Jackson. How afraid she'd been of revealing her fear, her insides nothing but deltas of panic and worry. She'd withheld herself beyond reason, never quite kind, never quite supportive, affectionate only when they were sick, when fevers and colds had changed the color in their cheeks, the shape of their eyes, their mouths turned quiet and helpless. They didn't seem like her children then, no longer resembling their father or behaving like sisters who fought day and night with few breaths between, and it was then, *only then*, that she would stroke their hair and kiss the warm tops of their heads, illness and febrile sleep affording her the right to say, *I love you.*

"It wasn't always this way," she said to the empty room, as if they'd gathered at the table, daughters and granddaughters under the same roof for the first time. She wanted to tell them about the winter before Jackson was diagnosed, when nothing more than a few spasms in his leg had caught his attention, nothing to stop Elin and Kate from climbing all over him every time he sat down. He and Vivvie bought a new sofa and chairs but still preferred the outdoors, especially evenings in winter, wool blankets like ponchos shielding them from the chill on the porch swing. One night Jackson hummed an old song from when they'd first met in high school, but he couldn't recall the name of the song or the words past the refrain. Vivvie tried but was unable to retrieve any more than Jackson, so they let that one go and began to harmonize another, but they came up short again. The bigger picture was that neither could remember an entire song, not these songs or any others, from the days before they were parents, as if it wasn't until after their girls were born that their life together had truly begun.

"Here we go," Jackson said, and began singing "Bye, Baby Bunting." Vivvie laughed and sang, "Daddy's gone a hunting," and they carried the tune with the seriousness of an anthem, all the way to the very last line, "A rosy wisp of cloud to win, to wrap his baby bunting in."

"What does that mean?" Jackson asked. "A rosy wisp of cloud to win?" They dug for an answer—historical references, symbolism, a scholarly discussion of a nursery rhyme. It was only when their laughter exploded that they finally quit, and Jackson stopped short and said, "I do believe I love you more than I did yesterday," and Vivvie said, "Isn't that a song?" and he said, "Probably," and she asked him to sing it but he didn't know the words.

Vivvie smashed her milk glass in the sink, busting it to pieces against the stainless steel. Time was nothing. Jackson could crawl inside her mind and the years would evaporate into weeks, weeks to days, days to seconds, until he was alive again, until he was dead again.

The silence of the house without her granddaughters was like a bully forcing her back to a wall. Vivvie flipped on the radio as if other voices could force it out, but that local gal's song was playing again, "Gull on a Steeple," and Vivvie didn't want to hear a sad ballad about falling into the past, returning to the one she loved. She shut it off and the silence was replaced by a hard wind, whistling, flapping the screens.

A small knock at the door sent her scrambling after the broken glass. She tore a paper towel from the roll and used it to scoop the shards into the trash, her gut filling with a sickly excitement that maybe it was Kate. Maybe this hospital business had been a misunderstanding. They were about to come to their senses, all of them, but Vivvie and Kate for starters, right here, right now, with Vivvie taking the first step, drawing on whatever courage she owned to speak about Jackson. No more pretending as if he never existed, no more behaving as if memories of him were so bad she couldn't speak his name. "I've been wrong about everything," she would say, "I ruined all that was entrusted to me," and that would be something. That would make all the difference.

The wind jerked the door when Vivvie opened it.

"Storm's coming," Wink said. The sky curled in shades of grey and green at his back, the air taut with electricity.

"I see that," she said.

"Supposed to be bad. The tropical storm is now a hurricane, just off Cuba." He pinched a sewing needle between his forefinger and thumb.

"What's that?"

"I got this splinter. Got a few of them stuck inside my hand. I can't see good enough to get them out."

"I didn't hear about the storm," Vivvie said.

"Category one."

Another gust yanked the door. "Get on in here," Vivvie said. "Before you get swept away."

Wink had never been inside, not like this, no deeper than reaching for a glass of water in the doorway, but one wouldn't know it by the way he fell back into the sofa when Vivvie gestured toward it. He relaxed in the corner, foot over knee.

Vivvie lit the orange lamp at his side and Wink leaned toward the light, picking at his hand.

"Scoot on over and let me have that needle," Vivvie said.

Wink did as he was told and Vivvie sat to his right in the corner, drawing his hand across her lap, firmly beneath the glow so that his upper body arched across her. "What were you doing with that stick?" she asked. "You must have a dozen splinters in here."

"Making a whistle."

"A whistle."

"Nothing wrong with a whistle."

"What do you need with a whistle?"

"I didn't say I needed one."

Vivvie dropped her head to the side, rolled her eyes up toward his face, inches from her own.

"My hands are soft," he said. "If they were rough those splinters wouldn't have been able to get in there."

"Are you bragging or apologizing?"

Wink smiled just enough for her to smell mint on his breath.

This was the first time she'd held a man's hand since Jackson was alive, the first time she'd been this close, and her skin tingled with the heat of nervous sweat.

"I thought your granddaughters might like a whistle. I planned to make two but they may have to settle for one."

Vivvie pressed her back into the sofa, widening the space between them. "Did you finish it?"

"There's a little more to it than I figured."

"I hadn't guessed."

Vivvie freed more splinters, lowered her lips close to his palm, and blew the slivers from his skin.

"Thank you," he said.

Vivvie nodded and continued digging.

"How's their mother doing?" Wink asked.

Vivvie's hand slipped, Wink jerked, and a drop of blood gelled in his palm.

"You're dangerous," he said with a smile. "First the snake and now me."

She placed his hand on his lap, handed him the needle, and stood. "I'll grab a tissue," she said.

"Well. All right."

The bathroom mirror revealed what a sight she was—mussed hair, smudged mascara, the lack of sleep around her eyes. She swiped beneath her lashes, ran her fingers like a comb across her scalp, leaned closer, and applied sheer gloss to her dry lips. She studied the reflection of her trembling hand. "My daughter is dying," she whispered, watching herself say it like watching a movie, a scene with the sole purpose of making her cry. She didn't cry.

She came back with peroxide and no tissue. She stopped in the middle of the room, intent on retrieving the box of Kleenex, but was held in place by Wink's smile. A moment passed and still she remained, as did he, smiling without asking anything of her, and another beat until it began to feel as if she'd meant to stop there all along and show off a new dress, offer him a drink so he could say, "Well, sure, darlin', there's nothing I'd love more."

But that wasn't it at all. What had really stopped her was seeing Wink from a distance, sitting in the same spot Jackson used to sit, the same place she found him months after his diagnosis, his legs already shaky, headed toward decline. He apologized for having been given such a bad break. Wasn't that what Lou Gehrig had called it? A bad break? But now that they knew what was coming he wished more than anything for a clean break. When she started to question what he meant, he said, "Please, Viv. Don't make me say it." Then he stared at her with a foreboding, a humiliation so deep it chased his tears back down his throat with such force that Vivvie felt her own airway squeeze shut. She understood that she would find him hanging in the shed. Or a bullet in his brain, or maybe he could get a hold of some pills, but find him she would—dead, in short order, no two ways around it. He was going to leave her. One way or another he'd be out of there long before they were ready, so what was the point in waiting for him to turn to stone? These were the cards they'd been dealt, he said, and the only question now was how they were going to be played. Were those final months of humiliation a reason to keep him around? Was it better for their daughters to remember him as a suffering, twisted animal unable to speak, sending Vivvie into crying jags, trying her patience and goodwill? Was there some point to saving him for the sole purpose of watching him die? "Tell me, Viv. Is waiting until our love no longer resembles itself, and *then* dying, going to serve some higher good?"

If she hadn't been robbed of her ability to speak she would have told him in that moment that she loved him more than all their days put together, loved him with a new kind of love, moonshine and life-blood, pure and wholehearted, so intoxicating it made her weak.

Outside, the coffee-can ashtray banged against the house and rolled away. The harsh scrape of metal on concrete set Vivvie's teeth on edge.

TWENTY

THE YOUNG MAN AT THE information desk had assured Elin that her sister was no longer in the ICU, and hadn't been for days. Her room was on the second floor now, where a plump, creamy-faced nurse, nearly half Elin's age, sat like a lifeguard atop a stool behind the nurses' station as if refusing them entry to the beach. She gazed at Elin, Averlee, and Quincy, standing in order of height on the other side of her station, and for a moment there was nothing but the buzz of fluorescent lights hanging low above their heads.

Elin gripped the counter. When she had mentioned going to the hospital to see their mother it was as if the girls had been awakened by a loud noise, stunned and animated, and then overjoyed to find themselves in the midst of some kind of celebration. "Please," Elin said to the nurse. "*Her own children* aren't on the 'no visitation list,' are they?"

The young woman shook her head and a trace of glittery bronze blush caught the light.

"Well," Elin said. "I can't very well send them down the hall to their mother by themselves." She sighed, ran her fingers through her hair, and crossed her arms, becoming her mother just then—the harried mood, the inability to suffer fools gladly, a sudden show of rudeness. She rubbed her temples.

"I could take them for you," the nurse offered, though her pinched stare gave her away.

"You're busy," Elin said.

"Yes. Very."

Averlee strained over the counter, her chin just inches above it. "Then pretend you never saw us," she said.

Elin gestured an empty palm toward her niece, her eyes still trained on the nurse, on the small grin the nurse seemed unable to contain.

Halfway to the hospital Averlee had asked to change into her new clothes. Elin had told her yes, of course, in the bathroom when they arrived, but now she'd forgotten the clothes in the car, and here stood Averlee, the frayed hem of her yellow shirt hanging loose, an eyesore, a judgment against her, or perhaps in her favor . . .

"Room 218," the nurse said. "But you didn't hear it from me."

Elin rested her hands lightly on the girls' shoulders as they walked down the hall, anxiety braiding her steps toward the unknown, and then toward the *known*, which felt a whole lot worse; all those old, pigheaded arguments now filling her with guilt, her hands on her sister's daughters, her sister/their *mother*, the person at whom Elin had hurled insults for years. She fought off the worming in her chest, the bile headed for her throat. It was one thing to bicker like siblings, all the shoving, bullying, competition. But something else, something sinister and base to wrap an ugly lie in a truth, to place it inside her sister's childhood heart where it could not escape, where it could only grow as she grew, Kate's own life's blood feeding it all the days of her existence.

The white buzz of fluorescent lighting penetrated Elin's skull, the long hallway zinging a tinselly white. She stopped at the water fountain, pulled her migraine prescription from her purse, and swallowed a pill. She came up for air, water dribbling her lip, orange bottle in hand, the girls watching her with a reserved kind of horror.

"Just *one*," Elin said, panting, wiping her mouth. "I get these headaches."

The girls pulled together like magnets.

Elin stuffed the bottle in her purse, peeled the girls' hands apart, closed them inside her own, and didn't let go until she rapped on door 218. She leaned her ear in but heard nothing. She pried the door open, slowly, like a thief.

Inside, the blinds were drawn, giving the L-shaped room a gloomy, brownish hue. The air smelled of green peas and coffee from an untouched tray on a stand at the end of the bed, the rest hidden around the corner. Steam rose from the white plastic cup. Before Elin could make a move, a teenage girl, a candy striper, if that's what they were still called, rushed in and grabbed the tray. "Sorry," she said. "I didn't realize she's only liquids." She disappeared and the smell faded to something yeasty, sour, dead.

The quiet room held a dense, droning weight, as if someone had just passed away, or was about to, and Elin recalled her mother's white catatonic face at her father's funeral, her lips slack with red lipstick she never wore. She didn't speak that day, didn't even cry. When she finally opened her mouth it was as if her vocal chords had been wrung between two fists, squeezing out the brightest tones, leaving behind an unpleasant brassy dullness that remained there to this day.

Elin stepped forward, peered around the corner, and covered her mouth. She'd entered the wrong room. A cadaverous-looking prop rested nearly upright in the adjustable bed. This was not her sister.

But Averlee was already touching the pale blue arm, the skin nearly see-through, a series of deep bruises on the back of her hand near the IV. "Momma," she said. "It's Ave."

"Me, too," Quincy said, moving beside her.

Elin's eyes continued to absorb what her mind could not fully comprehend.

Kate's head lolled toward her daughters, one eye peeling open, a twitchy smile sparking, fading, her bony chest beneath the neatly turned sheet rising and falling in wheezy, panicky, birdlike breaths. A whimper seeped from a throat so thin her small skull appeared large by comparison, her neck a loosely gathered knot at the base of a balloon.

Elin swallowed what felt like a cottony cloth down her throat.

Quincy patted her mother's shoulder. Again a flash of smile, chest fluttering, the whimper more pronounced.

"Girls?" Elin whispered. The room dilated with heat, a cool glaze of sweat peppered Elin's forehead. "I think she might need to rest."

Then a wet, sucking sound as Kate slurped at drool, coughed and moaned, her head barely slumping opposite now, toward Elin, her lids opened just enough.

Her inky eyes gripped Elin's skin like fingernails, gouging, and then giving her a good, hard shake. It wasn't madness, pain, or even anger that appeared to seize Kate. It was the look of affection, of generosity puncturing Elin's flesh.

Kate slurped, eyes blazing.

Should anything happen to me, who would look after my girls? What had Elin told her on the phone? *You disappear and then ask such stupid, shithead questions.*

Elin pulled a chair to the bed and sat, searching for words, any she could think of, rubbing her thighs but the sweat on her palms would not disappear. "So . . . I guess you wanted me to come," she finally said. "I'm sorry it took so long. I had to read between the lines."

Kate's throat jerked with laughter, and it *was* laughter, even as it sounded like a weary cat's mewl. Kate was laughing, and Elin laughed, too, but only a little, unsure if she had it right. Unsure if the joke wasn't actually on her.

Then Kate's laughter turned to coughing, choking, gasping.

Elin stood. "Is this normal? Is she okay?"

The look of despair in Averlee's face held no surprise, and Elin understood this was their life, their mother in varying stages of how she lay here today, though only last week she could speak well enough to phone Elin about the day at the beach, to pose the question about if something should happen to her, who would look after her girls. If something should happen to her. Christ.

Kate quieted, lids closed, a small grin pinned to the corner of her mouth.

Elin placed her palm on Kate's chest. Air moved weakly beneath the breastbone, and Elin withdrew her hand quickly, more from the reeling memory of a young sister on the beach than from the woman in the bed.

She turned and headed for the door, motioning for Averlee to follow. "Quincy, I need you to sit in that chair and keep an eye on your mom while I talk to your sister in the hallway."

Averlee started to speak. Elin held a finger to her lips. "We don't want to keep waking her." She gestured to the chair. "Two minutes, Quincy. I promise. You're big enough. You are."

Quincy's eyes narrowed and glistened in the dull light, like those of a wild animal about to bolt. But instead she crawled into the chair, glanced at her mother, at Elin, and then Averlee, who kept watch on her until the door closed behind them.

"We don't have a lot of time," Elin said. "I need to know what's wrong with your mom so I can help her."

"I don't know."

"How long has she been like this?"

"A long time."

"How long is long? A year, a month?"

"Kind of since preschool, I think."

Elin calculated backward. "Like, *four years*?"

Averlee shrugged, her eyes starting to well as if she had done something wrong. Elin softened her voice. "How long has she been really bad like this?"

"Mostly since Christmas."

"Christmas?"

"I guess so."

"Does she see a doctor?"

"Sometimes."

"Does she work?"

"Not anymore."

"How have you been living?"

Averlee didn't seem to understand the question.

"If your mom doesn't work, how does she take care of you, buy you clothes and food and stuff?"

Averlee shrugged. "The checks."

"What checks?"

Averlee shrugged again. "In the mail."

"Who sends them?" she asked, but she already knew. "What sickness does she have? Does it have a name?"

"I don't know any of that stuff."

Elin covered her eyes from the lights. "Can she walk?"

"Not anymore."

"Jesus. Do you all live with someone else besides your mom?"

"No."

"Then how did she manage? Was there anyone helping you?"

"The people from the center."

Elin dropped her hand and slowly opened her eyes to the pain. "What center?"

Averlee shrugged. "The center. They clean the house and get us stuff we need. They help her take a bath."

"Who *are* they?"

"People from the *center*."

"But what *is* it?"

Averlee dug her face into a frown.

"Oh, dear God. All right. You mean to tell me you *really* don't know what's wrong with her, I mean, she's never talked to you about how sick she is? She never said *anything* the night you had to call the ambulance?"

A spark of recollection seemed to flash across Averlee's face. She shook her head no.

"What did she tell you?"

"Nothing."

"That's not true."

"I already told you what she said."

"What did you tell me?"

"She said you like secrets."

"That's what she told you. *That* night?"

Averlee tightened her lips into something hard, practiced. She looked behind Elin as if someone were coming toward them.

Elin gripped her hair at the roots. The hallway was empty. "Come with me," she said.

When they returned to the room Quincy was standing near the bed in front of the chair, holding Kate's hand.

"Did she wake up?" Elin asked softly.

"Did she talk?" Averlee asked from the other side of the bed.

Tears spilled down Quincy's cheek.

"Great. See what you did?" Averlee said to Elin.

Kate lay undisturbed, even as Averlee's voice rose.

"What *I* did?" Elin asked.

"You made me go in the hall."

"I just needed to ask . . ." Oh, what was the point? Elin lowered herself, exhausted and heavy, into the chair. She gently pulled

Quincy onto her lap, wiped her tears with her palm, her cheek warm and soft as damp velvet. Elin wrapped her arms around her, closed her eyes, and drew in the scent of Quincy's strawberry shampoo.

Her eyes sprang open, her hands already reaching toward her sister. She secured the blanket at Kate's shoulder, accidentally brushing her collarbone, as cold and pointed as if unearthed from the ground. She tucked the covers along the length of her arm. Elin had never shown her sister such simple kindness. The one act of selflessness she'd offered her at the beach that day had haunted her ever since.

Kate's lids bobbed, eyes still wet and blazing with a heat already extinguished from the rest of her, even as her face appeared ice-bound, giving nothing away.

Elin brushed her sister's wrist bone, the back of her hand white and cold and smooth as marble, and it was then that Elin understood what was ravaging Kate's body. Not the name, but where it came from, and the fact that it ran through her sister's blood, and if Kate's blood, then her own, too.

The air bristled with cruelty. Her father's arms, too weak to be trusted, her mother's rising panic as he swung Kate one last time in the autumn sun.

TWENTY-ONE

THEIR MOTHER USED TO SAY they were nothing but sharp elbows. Nothing but quick tempers parceled into little bikinis. Nothing but house apes, or big-eyed Kewpies. When she said "big-eyed Kewpies" they knew they weren't in trouble. Not really.

But that day at the beach, when Kate and Elin were ten and eleven years old, their mother hadn't said much at all, reclined in her aluminum-frame chair, round-shouldered and silent, smoking and reading in the shade of her straw hat.

Elin and Kate weren't speaking either. Not after what Elin had said to her in the car.

Kate was busy shaping sand into a castle, her mouth an open pant beneath strings of wet hair. Elin glared at her through wavy bangs in need of trimming, wishing herself home, sketching in her notebook on the knotty-pine sleeping porch that Saturday afternoon, wishing they had never come to the beach.

"'How to Avoid Harmful Stress,' by J. D. Ratcliff," her mother read out loud from her magazine. She laughed a little and flipped the page.

Elin drove her toes into cooler sand. She tugged the vane of a gull's lost feather, carefully, the translucent barbs about to split like lips opening in slow motion. But then a hand swooped past her face and the feather disappeared.

Kate skewered the feather into a mound, humming to herself, packing sand around the pearly stem.

A burst of wind swept off the ocean and the air smelled of fish, of salt and seaweed baking in the sun, and then of Kate's fruity shampoo as her hair lifted beneath Elin's nose. The wind turned back with the scent of steamed hot dogs from the Snack Shack where the road T-boned the beach. Seagulls floated in circles, squawking as if to let Elin know to stop, do nothing, there were plenty more feathers to go around. She wanted this day to be over. Her skin tight, itchy, and hot, every crease in her body lined with clumps of gristly sand.

Her mother sighed and lit another cigarette. Baby oil had seeped into her calves, her skin a coated sheen of plastic-looking hide. She pecked her magazine and clicked her tongue. Ash fell into the spine. "Come on, girls. It's time to get this stuff picked up and get on home." She tossed the magazine into her bag, stood, and gestured her cigarette at the yellow buckets and Fresca cans at their backs. She glanced at her own things—chair, beach bag, baby oil screwed into the sand. "Easier said than done," she said, and Elin didn't know if she was talking to them or the magazine.

Kate dropped her hands, leaned back onto her heels, eyes squinting toward the ocean when she said, "I'm not done."

"Too bad." Elin came to her knees.

"I'm not done."

"It's time to go," Elin said.

Kate jumped to her feet and kicked in her castle. The feather slumped sideways in the sand.

"What'd you do that for?" Elin asked, but she knew.

Kate bolted toward the water, and the air had the same sharp feel as the time she ran away into the woods behind their house where their father died. Elin and her mother found her slapping at mosquitoes in the fork of an oak tree. By then they were all smacking mosquitoes, which was enough to shove their mother's temper straight into what Elin and Kate called *code red*. She jumped to grab hold of

Kate's foot. She pulled her, kicking and screaming, and Kate fell to the ground, the wind knocked from her chest. She couldn't speak when their mother raised her to her feet by her hair. Not even when she walked her home across the field the same way.

And what had Elin told her shortly before she ran into the woods that day? To the one place Kate knew their mother refused to go? What words had Elin whispered so crisp and clear, pure as truth, even as the whole of it spun straight from her imagination? *Mom killed him. Out there, in the woods. The blood on the dog's head. He must have been standing right next to Dad when she shot him. That's the real reason she gave Big Boy away. The real reason we aren't allowed to have another dog.*

Elin yanked the feather from the sand and crushed it inside her fist. It might not have been blood on the dog. He was always running off, dragged around by his nose, tearing into neighbors' garbage, into rabbit holes, bitten twice in the face by a snake. Or maybe *that* was it, real blood from a snake he'd lashed to death between his teeth.

You can't tell or we'll all go to jail, Elin had told her.

"Where do you think you're going?" her mother now yelled after Kate.

Kate didn't slow.

Her mother held her hands like a megaphone. "Get back here!"

Elin twisted and snapped the feather until the barbs were tangled as hair.

"There's sharks and stingrays out there!"

Kate's long hair whipped down her back like strands of a shredded cape.

Her mother pulled her straw hat off and scratched her hair free. "Go get your sister," she said.

Elin jerked her head up.

"You heard me." She pointed to the water. "Go on."

Elin threw the broken feather into the sand and stomped toward the waves. Kate had already hurled herself over the surf and disappeared. Elin stood on shore, thinking she could still turn back, that her sister couldn't stay out there forever, so what was the point? The warm, frothy tide lapped at Elin's feet. Not far down the shore a dog with speckled paws and white-tipped ears rose onto all fours and barked in Elin's direction. He licked the stiff hairs around his mouth and barked again. A man in cutoffs told him to shut up.

Elin glanced at her mother behind her. "What'd I say?" she yelled, and Elin waded forward and then dove in.

Saltwater tightened her face when she popped up and squinted against the sun. From the corner of her eye a flurry of her sister's hair swirled and disappeared beneath the water. Elin's arms and legs dangled in the nothingness, the tips of her toes journeying farther from the bottom than they'd ever been.

Her mother gestured from the shore like a coach signaling players to move faster, move that way, *go*!

Elin groaned through sideways strokes, a talent she'd perfected through years of swim lessons. Kate had disappeared again, and Elin's chest began to ache against the bone. When she stopped to catch a breath the water's depth was colder at her feet.

Her mother hollered some kind of threat and it sounded as if she and the speckled dog were now miles away, both barking at the same time.

Then something fleshy, something long and stringy brushed her arm and she screamed and jerked, but it was Kate, appearing on the surface, her slick hair clinging like a shiny black veil down her face. She blew water in Elin's eyes when she let go of her breath.

Elin rubbed her lashes and spit. The muscles around her elbows burned. She shoved water at her sister with the heel of her hand. "Stay here for all I care, Miss Freak. I'm going back."

Kate's laugh bounced off the water. Before Elin could say anything, her sister gulped a mouthful of air and dropped her body beneath the surface.

Elin's hand was quick as a trap. She caught Kate by the ankle and refused to let go, even as the strength of her sister's long leg pulled her beneath the water, where a heel struck Elin's jaw, making a crack inside her head, a streak of hot pain in her ear. She threw punches against the weight of water as if they were fighting at home or in the backseat of the car. The skin of her sunburned shoulders tore beneath Kate's nails and burned in the salty water. Tangled beneath her sister, Elin did not know which way was up, and swallowed gulps of water every time she screamed.

Then nothing. Nothing between her fingers, nothing against her skin. Only water rearing and shifting like a giant, angry eel. Kate was gone, replaced by a riptide, twisting Elin even farther into the dark and gushing cold. Her head struck the top of a sandbar as the ocean rumbled like thunder past her ears. This was it. This was all her life will have amounted to. One last fight with her sister. Her throat clutched in the middle. How long did she have? What did they say in swim class? *Don't panic.* How would she find the surface in all this darkness? *Don't panic.* Her heart would burst into a hundred pieces. Her skin shred into fish food. *Don't panic.* Any moment her fingers would claw into sand.

When the freshness of air rushed her chest it burned like wildfire throughout her whole body, and at first she thought she'd opened her lungs to the ocean. But it was air. *Air!* She sucked it in and coughed it out past the lining of her throat with a force that caused her teeth to ache.

She hacked and burped what felt like a rubber ball from her throat, then another, retching, spewing flecks of potato chips. Her body sloped, floating toward the shore, her mind registering nothing but the expanse of blue sky, the lap in her ears.

A man in a white paper hat appeared, hobbling out toward her. He swam in shorts and a T-shirt, hustling to scoop her into his arms. The paper hat slipped off his head and floated like a handmade boat across the water. He was the man from the Snack Shack.

For a moment there was only the sound of his breath in her ear, water sloshing her shoulder, the ocean billowing her hair.

Elin's legs finally came down in the shallow water, wobbling on solid ground. She wanted her mother. The other mother, the one who cared for them when they were sick, the one who put washcloths to their faces when they puked, who smeared ice on their fevered lips. She wanted the mother who brought them blankets, tucked pillows at their backs, and watched them as they slept.

The man held onto her shoulders as she walked. He loosened his grip only after the ocean was a good ways behind them.

"You're all right now," he said, smelling of relish.

Her stomach hung inside her like a bulging bag of dirty water. She was going to be sick.

"Do something!" Cords of her mother's brown hair in the wind, the round shape of her body came into focus. She was kneeling, urging the dog's owner, his cutoffs dripping wet, to *do something, do something!* The dog whined and yelped as the man's body made an arc over something in the sand.

Sticking out beneath him were feet.

Kate's bare feet.

Elin's vision tunneled. She ran and didn't stop until she barreled into the man, knocking him sideways in the sand.

Her sister lay motionless, a string of kelp clinging to an eyelid. Elin snatched it away. No one tried to stop her when she plunged into Kate's chest, and no one stopped her when she plugged Kate's nose, put her mouth to her salty lips, blasted air from her lungs into her sister's—another and another, stopping only to shove her weight onto Kate's chest in a constant, steady rhythm.

"Where's the lifeguard?" her mother yelled.

Kate's face was pale and glassy beneath the layer of tanned skin. Her lips more violet than pink. Her mouth hung open as if her jaw had come loose.

Elin plunged into the soft, spongy give of her sister's breastbone as if she were burying Kate with every thrust meant to lift her back up. She gripped Kate's face, felt the edges of her jaw, lumps of molars under the skin. She pressed into her lifeless lips and blew.

"Please, God," her mother said. "Doesn't anyone else know how to do this?"

Elin raised back and slapped Kate's face, knocking her head to the side.

Her mother grabbed her arm. "What's the matter with you!" Her mouth a twisted tremble of lips and teeth.

Elin knocked her away. The man in the cutoffs yelled "Come on!" and thrust Elin's hands back onto Kate.

She bore down harder than before, harder than they taught her at the pool. Elin would take back what she'd said in the car, if Kate would just wake up, she'd take it back. It'd been nothing more than revenge for Kate hiding Elin's paintbrushes that morning, for calling Elin's teeth ugly, her drawings stupid, her face so disgusting a boy would never kiss her without puking out his guts. For this, Elin had waited an hour, waited until Kate appeared unguarded, laughing at a kid making a pig face in a station wagon passing on the freeway. Elin had leaned into her ear, whispered hotly that Kate was the reason their mother had killed their father. Kate had driven her to madness, Kate was just *that bad*, and wasn't it clear by now that this was *true*? Or was she too dumb to see how everything was ruined the minute she entered a room?

"Uhn!" Elin clobbered her fists into her sister.

"Stop it." Her mother curled forward. "Just stop."

Strangers had gathered. Voices blended into a single gasp. Long shadows darkened Kate's face.

"You're nothing but a mean—*uhn!*—rotten little—*uhn!*—*bitch!*"

Kate's mouth turned tense and round. Her throat jerked upward once, twice, three times, and seawater sprang into Elin's eyes and nose.

Kate rolled onto her side with help from their mother, whose eyebrows rose in astonishment, mouth gaping as Kate spewed stringy grey liquid into the sand. And then she coughed and choked and even said something in between that wasn't clear.

Her mother let loose a round of hysterical laughter.

Elin's ears ached. She wiped the goop from her face, and backed away through strangers' greasy arms and legs smelling of baby oil and coconut creams. Her temples felt crushed by fiery sharp jaws. Scratches covered her arms and hands from Kate's fingernails and there must have been more near her eye and scalp where Kate took a chunk of her hair. She braced her knees and stared into the sand. She held the pain in her head, her whole body trembling.

When she looked up between the bare legs of men and women who'd come to see what was happening, her mother was kneeling over Kate's vomit in the sand, saying, "That's my girl."

Elin shuddered.

"Oh!" Her mother's laughter was short, detached, stagey as an actress in a televised play. "You see?" she said. "What did I say? That's my girl. Everything's all right now. She's going to be just fine."

And with that Elin didn't feel the need to take back what she'd said. They were alive, and being alive made it seem as if nothing had happened, as if all the rest had been canceled out. To be alive was enough. It was everything.

PART TWO

TWENTY-TWO

KATE'S LIDS CLOSED, HER MIND trapped beneath the weight of her skull, but she could see "DO NOT RESUSCITATE" as clearly as if the form still lay on the kitchen table before her, the physician's sharply scrawled signature still wet with ink.

Billowing ghosts swam the length of her bed. Shadows recast sunlight, throwing it back like lamps flipping on and off, on and off, on and off.

"DO NOT RESUSCITATE" on the yellow sheet of paper, signed by Kate, her physician, attached to her living will.

This was all Kate's fault. She should have planned a better suicide. *A Better Suicide*, collected poems by Katherine Fenton.

If only she could laugh.

She wasn't dead. Not yet. *I Woke Up Alive*, by Katherine Fenton. *I Woke Up Dead*, by Katherine Fenton.

Her daughters were meant to find her asleep at the table, nothing more, no drama, no choking to death while they stood by helpless, just a call to Mrs. Pearl, the neighbor, or to 911 when they couldn't rouse her. She'd taught them to call 911. Kate was meant to be toted away on a gurney, neatly—her daughters never having to look at her again.

But . . .

Time had lost all shape.

Her mother's voice in the hospital. "She's not breathing on her own?"

Kate had clawed her way up to the surface. The dreary leaden weight of gravity, her lips dead minnows, her tongue and eyes thick black slippery pools of nothing. "Get it out, get it out." Her mind cobbling together the pieces. Survived. Hospital. Her inability to speak, not the disease, not yet. Just yesterday, was it yesterday? She could still form words, slurred past a charley-horsed tongue. A respirator in her mouth. Lungs whooshing. Frankenstein. *Get it out. Get it out.* She did not want her mother to see her like this.

Someone corrected the course, put her life, her death, back on track. The nurse? "DO NOT RESUSCITATE" Kate had told her, told someone. Maybe it was understood. Someone somewhere had understood.

The respirator now gone, Kate breathed in feathery wisps on her own. Air, a strange and spectral matter, the final substance she pulled from the world, nothing.

If only she could speak. This close to leaving for good, there were things she wanted to say. And laugh. She was dying to laugh. That was *funny*. It all seemed funny now. Crack up over a crackpot attempt at rushing herself out when she was already so close to leaving. What had been the point? Oh. She remembered. Believing she could control the world, a fool's mission, right down to the burning desire to manipulate the memories inside her daughters' heads. Play God. Leave them with visions of her own making. Infuse meaning into the murkiness of confusion, recalling a childhood from decades-old conversations. Painting the past was as futile as it was necessary to get right, which one could not, ever, get right. How many versions were there? Everyone attached to her own.

Still, Kate had planted the seed. Her daughters would look back someday, remember their mother was ill, and it would be tragic, yes, but at least Kate died in her sleep. Give them that. The peace of it. A died-in-her-sleep story. Kate was lucky, then, so would say friends at dinner parties, spouses, psychiatrists, her children's children, someday. She had not suffered long. No better way to go.

What pain had these doe-eyed daughters of happiness known before Kate became so ill? How had they suffered? A bad day at school? Wanting a toy, a dress, a book Kate could not afford? Never knowing their father, perhaps? No. Even there they were still better off. All the fighting had gone on when Averlee and Quincy were too young to remember it. This too was something she had spared them.

She'd spared them everything, but in the end the world had other plans. The world said, *Take it in doses along the way, or get it all at once, but get it, you will. And what a grand finale it shall be.*

Days, hours, minutes left for her, and if one were to ask, if only she could speak, she'd say her spirit was already pulling away like reams of red and yellow silk. Like flames. It didn't hurt. Not to worry. It didn't hurt at all.

Elin appearing at her bedside, her deathbed, like the start of a parable: Life, just before opening a door marked "Death," cracks the window and in rushes Purpose on a dazzling, shimmering wind, whipping together a razzmatazz of ten thousand threads until an entire picture is projected on the wall right next to Death's door, so that the dying might see what it all meant, might understand that this, *this* is what it was all for.

See.

What a gift. Elin's likeness to Averlee, like the grown daughter Kate will never see, but *did* see, today, at her bedside, her deathbed, a grown woman come back from the future to say good-bye.

Kate and Elin, a set of trapped birds, each in her own cage. Kate would release Elin if she could. She'd been trying for six years, disappearing so that her sister could continue to move forward through life, a life new and separate from Kate's. And yet, in Elin's face, her voice, Kate had seen what remained, the traces of misery.

Where had Elin, an eleven-year-old girl, found the courage to save her? Retrieved such presence of mind? Kate had yanked Elin's hair, shoved her underwater with the madness of a child who did not understand consequences, did not understand that death was death, did not understand *finality*, wanting only relief from Elin, relief from her life, from *their* life. And yet, if it hadn't been for Elin, Kate would have died that day, would have never given life to Averlee and Quincy, would have never saw them into being. Where had that eleven-year-old girl found such forgiveness? Kate had tried to kill her, and minutes later Elin had the capacity, the clear-eyed grace, to solder Kate back among the living.

TWENTY-THREE

TWO DAYS LATER ELIN AND her mother brought Kate home. There was nothing in her directive that said they could not, only that no one interfere in the natural progression of her decline.

Now Elin wandered the crisp, spare rooms of Kate's white clapboard house at the end of Caldicott Street. She drew back the drape and gazed onto the meadow next door. *Meadow*, so Midwestern, so pastoral. Never had she thought of a grassy open field in Florida as a meadow. But the side-by-side rope swings dangling from the twisty, monster-thick branch of the live oak, the swing's silvery driftwood planks, and behind them tall grasses, violet wildflowers, two identical leathery-leaved orange trees, evoked an easy idyll of Averlee and Quincy scissoring back and forth in the shady mornings before the sun was too hot, chattering aloud all they would share only with each other, in this meadow.

She'd removed her shoes at the door, following Averlee and Quincy's lead, the shiny cinnamon floors deserving respect, and now the bare soles of Elin's feet gently stuck to the polish; the wood creaked when she stepped room to room, brushing objects with her fingers in passing. A white cereal bowl, a palm-sized ochre-painted wooden top, a tarnished handheld mirror—pieces of her sister's life pulling together like clouds, painting an expansive, foreboding scene.

The furnishings—wood, wool, Shaker-style elegance, everywhere a tidiness that gave Elin an uneasy jolt, stinging her with a new kind of shock. Nothing, down to the smell of rosemary in the window-sill, appeared the way she'd imagined—some version of chaos in a two-room bedlam apartment on the east side of town, Kate living off tips and little else. But here was a lustrous cedar-shingled cottage filled with bright white walls and sheer lemon drapes. Handmade quilted throws on the sofa back, a small sheepskin tossed over a royal-blue cotton chair, a grey wool rug in the center of the room, where Elin demanded Fluke stay to keep his claws off the gleaming fir floors. An aesthetic created with intention. With simplicity and grace. This was no accidental life thrown together, no last-minute ditch to make the best of running away. Kate's home was put together, step by careful step, with the deliberateness of love.

How had she done it? Where had she found the courage in the shape she was in? Elin searched for a single sign of Neal—razor, shoes, firehouse gadgets, his lock knife, seat-belt cutter, voltage detector—but there was no trace of him, or any man, in the house.

Mrs. Pearl had followed them to the door the morning they arrived with the medical transport team, holding it open as if she lived there, her face clearly pained as they wheeled Kate past on a gurney. Mrs. Pearl had rented the house to Kate, she said, unfurnished. This past year the lawn and all Kate's shopping and care were done by the local ALS foundation—the *center*—and with that in mind Mrs. Pearl looked at Elin and her mother above her glasses, a judgment cast against their lack of involvement in Kate's life. Elin restrained herself from saying, "This was not our fault," the glare from Mrs. Pearl aimed mostly at her mother, until Elin stepped forward and caught it like a sword to the chest. "Thank you for everything," Elin had said. "We'll take it from here." She stopped short of pushing her out the door.

Books lined the shelves on either side of Kate's tall bed, the headboard behind her made of long pine planks as if pulled from a saloon.

Stacks of worn notebooks filled a shelf to the right, and Elin guessed that Kate would have been forced to stop writing in them long ago.

She lay in the middle of snowy-white bedding, her shrunken body propped against half a dozen pillows. If not for the strain and guzzle of her breath, her dark waxen hair spilling and swirling into so much white gave the appearance of a child falling into a snow bank, readying to make an angel but instead falling asleep.

Now that Elin understood that this was where Kate had been hiding—not so much hiding as living, not so much living as plodding toward her death—she stood at the foot of this tiny woman's bed, held in place by an emanating, delicate innocence. Her sister was a stranger whose life had existed outside of Elin's understanding, hidden from her affections, an outsider with a warmth and affection all her own, uncloaked inside this house, broadcast in everything around her, the faces of her daughters the most staggering display.

TWENTY-FOUR

NANCY, WHOSE LAST NAME ELIN immediately forgot upon hearing, was a fiftysomething, rosy-faced hospice nurse with the tall awkwardness of a teenager. She read news magazines in the chair in front of Kate's notebooks, and every now and then gave her full attention to Kate's pulse. "You'll know she's close when her energy shifts," Nancy said. "That's not mumbo jumbo talk. That's what happens right before they pass."

She hadn't meant to be coarse. Elin understood this. Guiding the living and the dying toward the other side was complicated work. What a thing to do.

"Thank you," Elin said.

"And the coloring," Nancy added. "The blotchiness of the hands."

Elin slid her hands into the back pockets of her jeans and nodded at the window, at another summer storm gathering to the west. The air conditioner ran nonstop, the house cool and comfortable, and yet Elin had the urge to open the window. She couldn't explain why this was, nor did she understand her reluctance to act on it. A superstition? An old wives' tale of opening windows—or was it keeping them closed? Birds flying in and out of windows, flouting death. What did it matter? They were beyond bad luck here.

She had spent most of the day alone with Kate, or with Nancy near the bed, but now here was her mother—whose avoidance had been noted—inserting herself in front of Elin, and wedging open the window. A pressure, like that of a slit tire, released from the room. An earthy scent of far-off rain seeped past the screen. This seemed to be all her mother came to do. She was nearly out of the room again when Nancy called to her. "It's likely they can hear everything we say up until the last moment. Good to keep that in mind."

Her mother froze in the doorway.

Memories, like trick candles igniting long after Elin had snuffed them out. "I saw the dog's head the day Dad died," Elin had said, a teenager then, an adolescent enraged over something trivial and since forgotten, but the mention of the dog as clear as if she'd spoken the words now in Kate's room. "You rinsed it off with the hose," she'd said.

Her mother had ceased drying her hands at the sink and sat across the table from her. "Funny you would remember that. You were so young. But you're right. He got into a fight with a snake."

"Must have bit him hard."

"I guess it did."

"Is that why he was covered in blood?"

Her mother returned to the sink. "Yep. Stuck his nose in a snake hole and got bit." She leaned hip to hip, shifted the soap to the opposite side of the sink. "That's what happens when you stick your nose where it doesn't belong," she said.

Elin had stood near the table, staring at the outline of her mother's shoulders at the sink, and then she walked out of the house, fists at her sides, a light rain ticking her face. She wanted only to keep moving, the weight of their conversation at her back, the air she cut through thick and moist as a swamp, birds screeching in the green-leaved walls all around her. The impact of what Elin had said, what she'd *meant by it*, scratched at the surface, but she would not allow it all the way in. Ten minutes later the rain had swelled, pelting her arms and chest with a burning, stinging chill, and she did not care.

She gripped the hem of her tank top, pulled and twisted, nervously wrung it as she wandered in flip-flops, taking streets she'd never been down, miles from her home. She didn't know where she was, all the houses unfamiliar, the yards between them sparse, dogs yapping at her from behind windows, and somewhere someone practicing a French horn.

She turned for home after an hour. There was nowhere else to go. Teeth chattering, lightning striking all around her. The accusation. The *horror* inside it. She knew what she *saw*, understood it was bad, but what was she accusing her mother of? Say it. Say it out loud! Rain dribbled into her mouth and she could not utter a word, not then, not ever, not even when she'd said it to her sister when they were younger did she believe it was really true. Her mother killing her father would not solidify into a fact inside her head, could not come full circle as a truth. And why should it? What reason could she have had to do such a thing? If there had been fights between them Elin had no memory of it. If he had been mean to any of them she had no memory of that either, not so much as a single raised voice. And in all the years since his death her mother never said a word against him. But none of that mattered anyway, because if her mother was going to claim the dog had killed a snake that day, that their father was accidentally killed by some hunter, well then, *that* was the story, so where was Elin to go with her suspicions? The police?

The porch light was on and the door unlocked when she arrived home. Her mother's bedroom door was closed but a light shined underneath. Elin's ankles were coated with mud, and her head was starting to bite, all the way down the right side of her face.

Kate was off somewhere, her absence always a comfort, a relief to Elin's head as if a high-pitched ringing had stopped after days of badgering. Elin shucked her wet clothes into a sopping pile on the carpet between their beds. She didn't care. She didn't care what her mother had to say about that. She was shivering, crawling naked under the blankets, filthy feet and all, when her mother appeared in the doorway.

"Are you all right?" she asked.

Elin nodded, and then, "My head is starting again."

Her mother walked away and returned with a hot water bottle, a glass of water, and a pain pill.

The only thing Elin remembered after that was waking in the middle of the night and sensing Kate asleep in the dark across from her, the wet clothes gone from the floor, the glass of unfinished water on the nightstand where her mother had left it.

Now here was her mother in the doorway, her back to Elin, shoulders tensed in the way she'd been at the sink that day. She hadn't said anything wrong in front of Kate, hadn't said anything at all, and surely that was Nancy's point: that her mother understand there would be no second chance. Whatever needed saying, whatever Kate needed to hear, had to be done while there was still time.

Her mother dropped her hand and continued into the kitchen.

TWENTY-FIVE

VIVVIE HAD LOST HER VOICE. The ability to speak was still there. She wasn't sick, not like that. She just couldn't locate the words to release the cluster of emotion caught in her throat. So she busied her hands, food taking the form of remedy, of support for the living, for looking after the girls.

She fried chicken, baked potatoes, tossed a salad with carrots and apples, thinking of what kids ate these days compared with what they *should* be eating. She thought about the harried or blank-faced mothers emptying their carts onto her conveyor belt, Vivvie's whole adult life given to this exchange, the unceasing beep of a scanner the soundtrack of her days, cash in, cash out of hands, the drawer, boxes and bottles stuffed into bags, *have a nice day* the only thing separating her life from a factory worker's. It was over now. She would not return to Roth's, would never again stand behind a register. She was done with that life. Just as Kate would never shop for her daughters again, never bathe them, never make another daily decision about their lives. Those things would be left to others, and right now Vivvie controlled a salad with apples and carrots.

But she'd also enticed her granddaughters with a box of cake mix, jiggling it like a small threat that if they didn't eat their dinner they wouldn't get the cupcakes. They agreed to clean their plates. Of course they did. She'd set the box on the counter and wondered what the hell difference it made, and how cruel she was, demanding anything of these children on the eve of becoming orphans.

If a palm reader had told her last week that her life would change completely within seven days, Vivvie could not have dreamed a world of this scale. Her imagination would have captured a lottery win, a new car, even an all-expenses-paid weekend trip to the beach would have been a stretch, but never could she have imagined this.

The day had passed like a slow dream filled with dim rooms she didn't recognize, with people she knew who no longer resembled themselves, and all the while a constant pressure like a physical force funneled her forward, prodding her to do the right thing. What was the right thing? It became increasingly difficult to catch a waking breath in that house, as if a droning compression were forcing the oxygen outward, sealing it inside the white paint. It was nearly intolerable by the time she'd opened the window in Kate's room, sensing that was the source. An old wives' tale—the dying needing a portal to escape, the long-dead arriving to guide them away.

Vivvie didn't believe a word of that stuff but she'd opened the window anyway and felt a whole lot better for having done it, until Nancy said the thing about last chances for the dying to hear what needed to be said. Saying the wrong thing and not being able to take it back would be a lot worse, but Vivvie didn't say that, or anything else. Instead she returned to the kitchen in deep, careful consideration over what she wanted to say and if that was the same as what she *should* say and if either was what Kate *needed to hear*. But then Nancy was following her with that achy-looking walk, her burden doubled and clear, days spent in unfamiliar chairs, waiting for someone to die.

"She's awfully close now," Nancy whispered near the stove that Vivvie was preheating for the cupcakes. "I'd be surprised if she lasts through morning."

Vivvie nodded at the gas burners, and then she was in motion again, wiping the fridge, taking out the butter. She gripped the oven handle and dropped her head, hiding her face, hiding the tears that would not come. When she looked behind her, Nancy had already slipped away.

Now Vivvie had gone outside to the tree swings, and, sitting sideways in one, her feet up in the other, she smoked a cigarette with such need it was hard to believe she'd just smoked one ten minutes before. How dare fate bring her daughter home for just one day, this child, this baby she had grown inside her, spewed and billowed into life after twelve violent hours of labor. "Uncommon for a second child," the doctor had said, just short of worry. "A hesitant beauty," he'd called her when she finally arrived, her cheeks scorched red from screaming. "And disappointed in the world already." He laughed.

They'd shared the same blood, the same source of life, and yet Kate's tiny body had already contained the poison now killing her, Jackson's DNA inside Vivvie and Kate at once, an invisible illness Vivvie had so carefully nurtured into being.

As helpless as someone tied to a tree. That was how Vivvie felt, like someone waiting on a firing squad. Helpless as the time Kate ran off into the woods and Vivvie had called after her for two excruciating hours, anger and panic raging, bargaining and threatening in her mind and out-loud bursts as Elin trailed in silence behind her. Then came the sound of smacking in the same moment Vivvie spotted a red shirt in the fork of an oak. Kate covered in mosquitoes, swatting her arms, legs, and face. Vivvie fell to her knees, useless buckling bones, soft as paper, and down she went, pretending in front of Elin that she'd tripped. When she came to her feet she held her heart, so knotted, so beaten and battered she feared it would give out before reaching home, and both of her girls would be left there, swallowed by the woods in the dark.

Kate's face against the leaves, the sky beyond—she'd never looked more like Jackson than in that moment, and less than a mile from where he died. Vivvie grabbed Kate's ankle and tore her from the tree. Kate walloped the ground, a single grunt shoving the air from her chest, her eyes enormous in disbelief, her mouth open, no tears, just a panic-stricken child at her feet, and still Vivvie wanted to beat her into the ground. She screamed instead, an animal's rage filling the forest, howling with fists against the side of the tree.

Elin backed away down the trail, nearly forgotten until Vivvie pulled Kate to her feet by her hair, and Elin rushed forward, arms out as if to save Kate from their monster of a mother. But one look from Vivvie stopped her in her tracks.

By the time they'd stumbled free of the woods, the air was so black they might have fallen into the sky, the ground unsteady beneath Vivvie's feet. The only light an acre away in the dim glow from the bathroom shining down the hall. What if Vivvie had taken her girls into her arms right then, right there where a bonfire once burned, where their father had remembered how deeply he'd loved their mother by a river?

Kate refused to explain why she ran into the woods that day, but Vivvie had always suspected it had something to do with Elin. Kate was in some way protecting her sister, an occasion so rare and fragile that Vivvie would not allow herself to even think on it for fear of needing to get to the bottom of it, and thereby severing the flimsy cable binding one to the other.

Just one of so many regrets. Vivvie should have tried to understand, let the rope fray through her bloody hands if it meant that she might have somehow relieved Kate of her misery, interrupted her deep-seated desire to escape, to try, repeatedly, to return to the mysterious place from which she came.

Kate seemed to have been intuiting the inevitability of this day all along, trying to head it off by losing herself in the ocean, and in the forest where her father died, and in the bathroom with a razor blade, the kitchen with pills that had brought her all the way to death's door but had not fully opened it, not yet, but very, very soon. Kate was about to walk out for all of eternity, no matter the wishing, the bargaining with God, no matter the bigger picture of reason, *this was now going to happen*. Tomorrow she'd be gone, the day after that, too. Another death, another set of young daughters left in its wake.

Vivvie dropped her feet to the grass and smoked and smoked. She wished she could speak about these things with Elin. Vivvie had told her own mother most anything, her mother more like a friend, offering laughter instead of advice in the years just before she died. Why did everything have to go unspoken between Vivvie and Elin? Unspoken but not unaware. Why did they feel the need to play this game of fool you/fool me that neither was winning or would ever win?

If things were different Vivvie would ask Elin why she never spoke her husband's name, never called him on her cell, even now, with all this going on, not one sentence about him, nothing to show she even *had* a husband aside from the ring on her finger. She was her mother's daughter. The great pretender. And it made Vivvie sick.

She blew smoke up into the tree and shook her head at all the thoughts she was having, at the strange, dusty feeling in her chest and eyes as if a dry heat had absorbed her spit, her tears, her spirit parched as kindling. Every drag heaved into one's lungs made life that much shorter. Wasn't that what they said now? Pictures of black lungs in doctors' offices. Every cigarette another hour or day or year erased from Vivvie's life, clear cold facts that never made her quit.

Vivvie flicked her cigarette butt into the grass and slid her palms down her thighs. The world did not owe her a thing. And yet she had the urge to tell a Lord she'd long stopped believing in that she recognized she ought to be grateful for having been given this day, like a gift she in no way deserved but willingly accepted, even though she could not feel its worth. Not now, not yet, not this offering or anything else, but surely there would come a day when she'd no longer be numb, and she'd recall what she'd been given, this day with her daughters, her granddaughters, gathered together this one and only day, and she would cry hot tears and give herself over to agony, and she would not be terrified by either.

TWENTY-SIX

ELIN'S MOTHER HAD BECOME OBSESSED with domestication of the highest order, her life's purpose apparently managing cupboards and a refrigerator, stacking groceries from Roth's, the counters gleaming, even as lunch, and perhaps dinner, simmered in white cast-iron pots on the stove. But now she was smoking on the children's swings, her lips shaping into words as if she'd gone crazy, as if she were speaking to ghosts.

Elin stopped watching, felt herself useless, idle hands and all that. Even her nieces had occupied themselves in subtle, low-tone beats in other rooms, with storybooks and dollhouses, sketchbooks on the living room floor, and in between playing quietly with Fluke, their voices floating sadly down the hall. "Oh, little puppy. Sweet little puppy boy, come here."

Another blue-black storm, like a puffed giant, was ready to howl and blow. Elin felt small inside her loose white blouse at the window, as misplaced as she'd ever been, incapable of doing what was needed, unsure, in any case, of what *was* needed. She couldn't protect her sister, or any of them against what was to come, and she supposed what she felt was hopeless, helpless. Utterly alone. Then she remembered—as if her marriage had happened decades ago in some forgotten country—that somewhere in the world she had a husband. She'd married a man with the intention of spending her life with him, he for her and she for him, a kind and loving buffer against the harsh edges of the world, a man so different from herself, their life together so unlike any she had known, that she could not help but forget all about the person she used to be. But how strange that all sounded now. And yet how *perfectly correct* it rang out when they began, how right the promise declared itself, a win-win deal cut and shaken upon, and everything that followed, everything built up and out around them was evidence of their agreement. And now? So soon, the marriage was already feeling past. And looking back she had no way of knowing if Rudi had ever actually loved her, or if he loved her still. What had he seen when he looked at her all those years? Had she ever allowed herself to be seen?

He had done them both a favor. She saw this now, evidenced by the pang of guilt she'd felt the other day. She'd been waiting for something to happen, waiting since the day they married, since she'd *branded* love like one of her accounts, slapped it with an identity, an easily recognizable logo. She'd been waiting for someone to come along and break it open, let the yoke ooze in directions unknown because that mess was where she was, all over the place. That mess was *who* she was, neither here nor there, and she'd been waiting for someone to free her from the neatly assigned category where she lived so tidily, dry as an egg shell, as Rudi's wife, waiting so she wouldn't have to bust it open by herself.

And yet, grief rolled like a tide toward her, grief for what she'd wanted it to be, for what it would never be, no matter the want. She was going to need a lawyer, her life about to head into overdrive on the lexicon highway of divorce law, something she knew little about, save the official term for their discord—*irreconcilable differences*—which surely they could agree on. Everything would be accounted for, the worldly accumulation of what had been their life, reduced to a list—business, house, cars, furniture, bank accounts, retirement funds, antique rugs, Tiffany lamps. Fluke.

Kate moaned softly behind her. Elin had briefly forgotten, slipped away from what was happening at her back. *Wake up and tell me what it's like to be divorced. Wake up. Wake up.*

Elin dropped into the chair, the whole of her a hot mess of convulsing sobs, which was how Nancy found her a short time later, and handed her a box of Kleenex, a tool of her trade. She kneeled and patted Elin's knee, which, surprisingly, soothed her.

An hour later Elin was alone again and the buttery scent of cupcakes had taken over the house. Kate's birthday was next month. She would turn, or would have turned, thirty-six years old. Elin held her hand, a semblance of small, white bones. According to Nancy, Kate could feel everything, feel and think and understand just like before, and Elin wondered if she could sense things, too, like Elin's sorrow. She wondered if regret could pass through her skin into her sister's, and, if so, would Kate intuit that Elin's marriage, at least in part, had been to prove a point? That part of the scaffolding that had held up her marriage was assembled by a one-upmanship, an in-your-face middle finger directed toward Kate, a competition of relief-from-the-past, that, until this moment, Elin had believed she'd won?

"Ah, hell," Elin said out loud. "Don't be so hard on yourself." It had all worked out in the end, hadn't it? Those two beautiful girls everybody's proof, everybody's reward?

A book of poetry lay on the nightstand. Elin leaned back and sighed. She glanced at the shelves, more poetry, novels, books on birds and plants. "Would you like me to read to you?" She lifted the book from the nightstand and it fell open in her hands to a page read many times, the spine worn in place, a poem about winter Sundays had been underlined and Elin began there.

Kate moaned, her right arm twitching.

Elin read that poem and several others before the rainstorm, a deafening racket, crashed against the roof. A sheet of drizzle on the windows distorted the dark outside, lightning flashed, and Elin placed her hand back onto Kate's, feeling the life inside her sister thin and cool as fog.

The lights flickered, and after a moment Fluke crept into the room, his whole body trembling. He'd been forbidden to leave the living room, and Elin wondered if his defying her had caused him more fear than the storm.

"Come," she said, and he hopped onto her lap. She held his warm body to her chest, and then she placed him next to her sister like a hot water bottle on the bed near her hip. She leaned and kissed the top of his nose, squeezed his small ears. Coffee was brewing in the kitchen. Elin could smell it, could hear the gurgle as the last of the water dripped through the maker. Evening had already arrived, the light now pewter-colored in the far corners of the room. A long night lay ahead, which must have been what her mother was thinking with the coffee, something to help keep vigil.

When Elin looked up Averlee was in the doorway wearing her cobalt-blue shirt and tan capris, a cupcake in her hand. Her face was hidden in the shadow of the unlit hall. Elin couldn't read her expression.

"Come here," Elin said. "Come sit with me."

For the next hour Elin held Averlee to her chest and gave her tissues and patted her knee. She could hear her mother in the other room playing a quiet game with Quincy, engaging her in a way she'd never done with Elin and Kate.

TWENTY-SEVEN

THE HOURS HAD LOST ALL shape. What day was it? What time?

Saturdays had been Kate's favorite. No school, no work, the girls up early, whispers from the living room, spoons tinkling cereal bowls Kate's weekend alarm. Late mornings swimming in the cold springs. Kate loved to swim. Even after what had happened with Elin, she loved the freedom water gave her, the buoyancy. And later, when it was no longer safe to get in, it was nearly enough to dangle her legs from the sideline, a hot slab of limestone heating the backs of her thighs, while her feet floated in what felt like an ice bath. Her daughters loved the water, too. Three sea creatures in the cold spring waters of Central Florida. Hot days diving into bottomless cold, fresh Plant City strawberries on the grass, a sloppy burger and chocolate shake on the way home. Wordless, exhausted car ride home, a silent, satisfied pleasure lasting into the evening, then showering away the grime, piling under overlapping blankets, the cool air conditioning slowly drying twisty cords of hair, a movie, caramel corn, pop.

If Kate had magic wishes she'd grant such joy to Elin. She'd offer her more than her own disappearance, selfless as it was—the most selfless act she'd ever offered her sister—but not enough, not even close. She was about to offer her so much more.

"Don't be so hard on yourself," Elin said.

Was Elin reading her mind? Had Kate spoken her thoughts out loud?

And anyway, look what had happened: Who could have predicted the applesauce jar? One day her hand could no longer turn the lid. Could not. One day. Just like that. One day it all made sense. Her father's feeble arms, legs, how quickly he was gone before he was *gone* gone.

And now someone was crying in the room. She'd rather they didn't. Please don't do that.

"Would you like me to read to you?"

Elin. Kate knew her voice, recognized the poem about no one thanking the father.

Mother.

Tick, tick, tick. Rain on the window. A clock. Her mother in the truck. Pistons ticking. Eagles. They were going to see an eagle in a tree.

Someone had turned on a lamp. Window black. The middle of the night. A flame. Not a lamp. A cupcake framed through the slit of an eyelid, a pure white cupcake, white tray on a white bed, the single candle burning. Kate's vision tipped. Thank you. Her mouth defying her wishes. Thank you. Her mouth humming. No sense. Nonsense.

A tickle. A movement, like laughter in her chest. Like choking. Swallowing a sharp chisel. A buzz, a razz.

The hours had lost all shape.

Her mother, her sister, her father. She missed them. Felt a four-year-old's yearning for their faces, arms, laughter, a giant all-encompassing yearning, guzzling her whole.

Forgive me. For God's sake, line up at my feet and forgive me everything.

Just like the poem, Kate had not understood the sober sacrifices of love. Then six years ago it became clear. Staying would have hurt them all, staying could only maim the spirit of the living. Staying was to be a stand-in for her father, for what her mother had done. Yes,

Kate had known all along, the way Elin knew. Knowing without knowing.

She had no choice but to disappear. She had never been fully part of the world in the first place, one foot in, one out. Only these past six years had she truly come alive.

Elin never even knew her, would never know Kate.

A mother.

A *good* mother.

Rosemary in her kitchen windowsill.

Notebooks full of poems.

A poet.

Elin never knew.

Never knew how she'd broken Kate's heart.

Never knew Kate understood that she'd broken Elin's, too.

Dear sister.

Dear mother. Oh, *mother*.

So attached to their versions of the truth.

TWENTY-EIGHT

ELIN'S HEAD FELL BACK IN the chair next to Kate. She watched the ceiling for a time and then closed her eyes and listened. Her sister's labored breathing, and in the living room Averlee and Quincy winding the wool throw into a bed on the floor again for Fluke, making him their doll, their child, their baby going to sleep. "Good puppy, good boy, good night, baby boy." The faucet gushed on and off in the kitchen sink, dishes clamored into stacks, and after that a broom scratched the wooden front porch with a rhythm that nearly put Elin to sleep. At some point a moment of silence fell over the house, even Kate's breathing seeming to falter, and Elin's eyes shot open, as if everyone had stopped and remembered at once.

Nancy's business card was a presence like the woman herself, there if needed but otherwise fairly unnoticed. It littered every surface—Kate's nightstand, kitchen table and counter, the coffee and end tables, natural places one might be standing or sitting after Kate passed away, and wondering whom to call.

When night fell Elin guided the girls through their bedtime routine of pajamas and teeth brushing, ordinary tasks carried out with eerie, gel-like movements. The world would not be the same when they woke, and their small bodies seemed to understand, articulating what their minds could not as they crawled, tenderly, beneath matching lavender sheets. Elin kissed their foreheads as Kate must have done, wished them sweet dreams as any mother would do, while quietly hoping sleep would at least come for them, knowing it most likely would not.

She hesitated near the door. Her mother had gone into Kate's room across the hall.

"I'm sorry," her mother seemed to say, though Elin couldn't be sure. "I love you," Elin thought she said, hoped she said. Elin slipped into the bathroom and waited until the wooden floor creaked where the hallway joined the kitchen before coming out.

She found a sleeping bag in the mudroom closet, and then passed her mother settling beneath a blanket on the sofa. "Good night, Mom," Elin said, but there was no reply. "I'll let you know if there's anything."

Elin unfurled the sleeping bag on the floor next to Kate. She crawled in fully dressed and lay awake in the dark listening to the soft rattle of Kate's breath. Fluke lay on the bed with Kate near her feet, everyone awake, everyone waiting.

"When I'm forty I'll be rich, married, have five kids, and live on the beach," Kate had said on the way to the beach the day she nearly drowned.

"When I'm forty I'll be rich, single, no kids, and live in the city," Elin had replied, and then came the station wagon with the pig-faced boy, and after that Elin whispered a feverish evil into her sister's ear.

Elin sat up, held her knees to her chest, and listened as bloated raindrops ticked the windows at intervals before disappearing.

"Remember when we caught a firefly in a jar and wished we had a tree house so the jar could be our lantern?" Elin said. The rare memory had pushed its way to the surface, rescued from before their father was dead. "Such logic. Wishing for a whole tree house just to put a lantern. Do you think we ever asked Dad to build us one?" What could he have said? What could he have felt? There were no memories to say.

Elin reached up and stroked Fluke's back and stared out at the night sky, wispy clouds pulling apart, starlight appearing with a fragment of moon.

The cupcake from Averlee sat on the nightstand and Elin opened the drawer and pulled out a set of matches she'd found earlier in the kitchen. She lit a candle on the cupcake and placed it on a white tray on Kate's bed, and the ghostly silhouettes in the room made Kate appear as if she'd already passed, her eyes sunken in shadow, hands coupled across her chest. But a meek rattling breath, a small gap of an opened eye said otherwise.

"I want you to know that I got over Neal years ago," Elin said. "I was just too proud to say so. That's not true. I was too *mean* to relieve you of any guilt you might have had."

Elin recalled how Neal had followed her from the house to her car that day as she piled in her bags, his look of disbelief, mouth gaping, palms open at his sides as if waiting for her to hand her stuff back. She'd kept thinking about what Kate had said, that there was no way he'd let her go. He would surely go after her. He never did.

"You don't even know where you're going," Neal said.

"Not exactly, but I have a good idea."

"This is crazy."

"Staying here is crazy. For me it is."

"Running away is not going to solve whatever's going on with you."

"I'm not running away. I'm running *toward* something."

"But I'm *here*, Elin."

How to explain? He didn't see her misery, her interior life a ponderous, blood-deep anguish, and maybe this too was what she believed Kate had understood about her, because she lived it in the same way. But here was a man who put out fires for a living, pulled mangled children from wrecks, siphoned scalding water from busted hot-water tanks, and he did not see the emergency in Elin's soul.

"Come with me," she said, and Neal, an only child of older parents long since dead, let slip his steadiness, his need for safety first. A risky adventure seemed to hook his imagination, an alternate, unknown future flashing behind his eyes. "You know you can get a job anywhere," she said.

"That's not true," he said.

"It's mostly true," she said, and watched as his steely, protective curtain returned, forever obstructing the view of the great wide open.

"Come back inside," he said. "Please. Just for a minute, so we can talk."

"I'll call when I get where I'm going," she said. If she'd gone inside he would have talked her out of it, out of her shorts and shirt, too. He would have prodded her with a reasoning that wasn't necessarily wrong, just wrong for her, but by then she would not see past it, not with him touching her, gazing eye to eye. "Maybe you'll have changed your mind by the time I get there," she said, still believing her sister without reason, believing out of want, but Neal turned away from her. How many destinies were altered when he slammed the door in her face? How many more when Elin got into her Volkswagen hatchback, trembling and weeping down Interstate 4 with the hurricane season at her back? She'd brought a copy of *The 50 Best Places to Live in the United States*, read it at rest stops, and four days later she arrived in Portland, Oregon, a place she'd never before been. How many more lives felt the ripple effect of that? How many reshaped, transformed, and undone?

A week after arriving, when she was at the base of Mount Hood, she'd slipped into the phone booth, barely able to contain her excitement. She knew what she needed to say to him. But as soon as he heard it was Elin on the line, she lost her voice, not because of what he said, but because of his silence, the wall of disdain so impenetrable, he could not absorb what she needed him to take in, which

THINGS WE SET ON FIRE

was that leaving had been such a simple, small thing, like stopping the car on the side of a road to take in a farmhouse, to study a tree on the side of a hill. Leaving had allowed her to think about the people who lived other lives in other towns, and to find her own life, because it did not exist in Florida, *she* did not exist in Florida, but she did now, in the west, come alive like an animal, roused and catalyzed through the wilderness.

"Come west," she was going to say. A line for a laugh, standing in the snow she was going to make him laugh. *Come west, young man.* She'd come down a mountain to tell him this, and to tell him that she loved him. *I've come down a mountain and it's snowing and I love you.*

But she said none of those things because he could not hear them. She did not know her sister had gotten to him first.

She said, "I hope you're all right."

"I'm seeing someone," he said.

Her chest barely had time to take the sting. "That was fast."

"Not as fast as you packing up and leaving. What'd it take, Elin? Two hours? Less? An hour to throw your clothes and books and albums in your car and disappear?"

"I'm sorry. I shouldn't have called. It was stupid."

"You think calling is the stupid thing, Elin? You think calling me is the *problem*?"

"Do I know her?"

"What the hell difference does it make?"

"I don't know."

"You don't deserve to know."

Elin was already crying quietly, hating herself for it, and for everything else she had no control over. Why she'd imagined it would be so easy, she didn't know. She was naïve. Before that moment she was. She suspected she wouldn't be after.

"I take that back," he said. "You *do* deserve to know. You actually do."

Years later it was like a memory that belonged to someone else, a story she once read about but had gone fuzzy on the details. So many times she'd thought to call and say the things she never said, but nothing good could have come of it. These were not sentiments to make anyone feel better. She never knew what Kate had told him. She stopped wanting to know years ago.

Hot pink wax hardened in the white frosting. Elin held her bottom lip between her teeth, forbidding more words from jangling loose. She was sick of herself, sick of clinging to old anger. Like moss gripping a rock, she wanted to kick it free, but oh how slippery it was.

"Happy birthday," Elin said as if making a toast, and Kate's hand twitched toward the cupcake. "Kate? Can you hear me? Make a wish. On the count of three I'll blow out the candle for you. Can you see the cupcake? I lit a candle for you. It's here on the tray. Make a wish."

TWENTY-NINE

KATE HAD SPARED HER MOTHER and sister her limp, her drool, her slow and ghastly decline. She'd spared them their own pathological past, and that was no small task. And yet she'd spared them the love she might have offered, too, a love she couldn't offer, a love they could not see anyway, no matter the want.

She had never loved her mother more than the day her doctor explained what was wrong with her hands, what would happen very soon, her doctor her executioner, detailing the workings of the guillotine. Had someone else in her family died from ALS? She'd answered yes without hesitation. Shivering on the cold examining table in the cool green room, fully clothed as if in ice, memories of her father snowballing through her mind. His weak hands, odd walk, her mother forbidding him to swing her. Dear mother. "Yes," Kate told the doctor. "Yes."

Knowing without knowing.

Nothing had ever quickened the life in her heart faster than her own impending death. She had no memory of leaving the doctor's office or how she got home that day. All she knew was that by the time she opened the front door of her old apartment, the future, her future, had nearly taken shape. The rest of her life would not be spent as a symbol of all that was wrong with her family. She would not open that door, invite the past to rush in, devour her own children before she was forced to abandon them. Quincy was only seven months old.

Two to five years, on average.

Kate had made it to six. Six more years with her daughters. But the day her doctor had told her her fortune, Kate went home and asked Neal to leave, something she should have done long before, made clearer by the fact that he grabbed his things without a fight, without a tear, without one single word. When Kate followed him to the driveway, saying, "I never loved you. This whole thing between us was a terrible mistake," he did not turn around and deny it. He did not say he'd wished it had been any another way.

One month later Kate called her mother to say she was leaving the state, getting out just like Elin, she just needed a little time, a change. She'd promised to be in touch once they got settled, and then she disconnected her number and moved across town. As often as once a week she returned, sometimes boldly, parking in Roth's lot. Two rows back afforded her a glimpse of her mother behind the large plate windows, ringing up groceries, a drawn face, smiling every now and then.

Three months later Kate couldn't be trusted to drive. And then she couldn't leave the house. But the Internet allowed her to find Elin's website. She read Elin's blog posts and links to design articles, and over time it began to feel like a conversation, like they were friends, sisters, chatting about art and poetry, about a life that mattered to them both.

Kate found Rudi's dealership, too, a headshot of him in the corner of the homepage. He was gorgeous, no other way to say it, more handsome than Neal, an old-world look, a classic beauty of a face. Kate was happy for Elin, until the day she clicked through the employee's names and faces, their bios, and a new photo gallery, where she came across a blond in a steely blue jumpsuit, glancing up at

Rudi, her eyes catching his *just so*, and Kate nearly gasped. She could not shake the feeling. She saw what she saw, and had been wondering for months if Elin had seen it, too.

"Don't be so hard on yourself," Elin said.

A cupcake.

Sugar.

Butter.

Cream.

I will blow out the candle for you.

Make a wish.

Kate traveling with Averlee and Quincy down the two lane truck route toward an eagle she'd never before seen. Look there, in the trees and in the smell of pine, and the sharp, wintery blue sky, a tenderness, how perfect the cool, cool day, benevolence in her bones put there long ago by her mother. Look now, Kate pointing at an eagle lighting on its thickly woven nest, as wondrous as an early morning trip to the mountains, yet so close, in the bright flickering flame, to home.

PART THREE

THIRTY

NEAL STOOD IN THE ARIZONA sunset for the better part of five minutes. His tin mailbox atop a weathered pine post burned his elbow, but he forgot, repeatedly, and leaned against it for support. The long envelope in his hand was slightly tattered and stained, forwarded from two previous addresses, postal stickers overlapping on the front. The return address was his cousin Angelina's in Orlando. He had not heard from Angelina since moving to Arizona six years ago.

The only other mail was an envelope written in his own hand, *return to sender* stamped red across the front. He did not open it. He began to shake.

He read the letter from Angelina, and then the newspaper clipping tucked inside, an obituary, and then he reread both once more, carefully, the fuller story blooming now, and his breath came up short. *Kate has died, succumbed to ALS, or Lou Gehrig's disease, which I'm sure you've heard of. Did you even know she was sick? If you get this letter, the law is looking for you. You're the only parent those girls have left.*

A drop of salty sweat stung his eye and he looked across the road at his house, his shiny yellow Karmann Ghia in the driveway, waxed yesterday, a rare thing for him to do, born of boredom, but now the polished finish made the brick house appear buttoned up, as if the people living there were smooth-sailing through their days.

He stuffed the envelopes in the back pocket of his jeans and wiped his forehead on his arm, itself damp with sweat, and he hurried across the red sand into the house, slammed the door, and leaned his back to it. Even when he noticed the trembling of his hands he could not make them stop.

Two imaginary daughters appeared, slumped on the sofa. "Hey, Daddy," one said, pointing the remote at the TV, and the other asking for dinner or shoes or whatever it was girls asked for, and, "My God," he said. Kate was dead.

He started toward the phone, a bubble of panic in his chest. Who was he going to call? He thought he heard the door, stopped, and looked through the blinds. A dust devil spun toward the oversized aloe lining the driveway. No one there, only the wind pushing red sand between acacias on the hill across the road. He was still sweating.

Did you even know she was sick? looped inside Neal's head with such force that he nearly spun the words out loud.

No. He did not. But knowing now was turning everything on its head, upright where it belonged all along.

He pulled the envelopes from his pocket, slapped them into his open palm, and stared across the living room into the kitchen as if daring someone to come toward him, though that wasn't how he felt. A guilty anger wove through his gut, an eerie charge for which he had no words, only the shape of a vague and sudden future forging through his mind.

All those letters he'd mailed over the years to his daughters, letters like the one returned in his hand, letters he was sure they never saw, and he wrote them anyway with the belief that one day Kate would change her mind, would sit the girls down and slide the stack across a table and explain how she'd held them back and how that had been a mistake. She would tell their daughters how Neal had sent news to them every month along with a hefty amount of child support ever since they were babies, and she would encourage them to sit together in a quiet kitchen and read each letter carefully. Their hearts would reshape with every word, all the worried little threads that had formed there over the years dissolving with each peak of insight until they came to rest in the long valley of understanding that life was not perfect, and not everything had been as they'd believed. Their father had loved them after all, his staying away dictated by this selfsame love.

And now Kate was dead.

A new kind of lonesome tore through him. Unlike the days where he felt he could not rise from his bed if another human being did not lay hands on him, if a voice did not whisper one small word into his ear, even to ask for a fork, a book off a shelf, unlike that, this new, godforsaken battering of hurt called for motion.

Through the house and out the back door he went to stand before a golden-purple sunset, the outline of a mule deer against the sandstone peaks before it disappeared into the cottonwoods. The vision of his grown daughters forgiving him everything vanished for all time. A tangle of new options fell as his feet, fractured and flimsy, impossible to hold, but he was certain that the lawn beneath his feet would become their yard, the mountains their view, the house at his back their home. It already had. He was their father. The only parent those girls had left.

THIRTY-ONE

ELIN WOKE ABRUPTLY, SUCKING AT the air, feeling as if something terrible was waiting, would always be waiting, on the other side of every new day. By the time she remembered where she was—her room at the B and B—and understood it was just after dawn, she was pulling away from her dream, a nightmare scurrying back into corners unseen.

Grief filled her bones like buckshot, painfully weighing her body to the bed. It caught in her throat every time she spoke, and on top of that, a gritty glue of anguish permeated her membranes—the lining of her sinuses, the tender bed of her fingernails. Every whiff of gardenia in the sun, every piss taken *hurt*—tugging with it a new layer of agony from some other crevasse it had folded itself into.

She lugged her body to the edge of the bed. Morning birds called to each other at the window. No sound from the girls asleep in the adjoining room. Fluke had slept at her feet. She was failing her own dog—no commands, no direction, no sense of purpose. She'd had him for five years, and in three weeks she'd made a lesser animal of him. They'd all, in one way or another, been reduced.

She couldn't bear to be in the house where her sister had died, couldn't bear to bring home the urn that contained her ashes, so it remained at the funeral home, where there had been no service of any kind per Kate's wishes. "I request that everyone should think on me quickly if they must think of me at all. Scatter my ashes in the ocean and get on with living."

When her mother took charge of Kate's estate, the girls fell under Elin's care, and she brought them here, where, within days, these ever-loving sisters began to fight.

Yesterday it was over who got to give Fluke commands, another sign that Elin had turned in her badge. When Averlee stepped in front of Quincy to make Fluke sit, Quincy shoved her, hard, sending Averlee to the floor, where she barely missed landing on Fluke.

The horror in Averlee's face equaled the horror of Quincy's tears, each bursting forth, a dam and an ineffectual cork. If they'd been any other kids their spat would have been forgotten, a few tears shed and left behind. But they were not other kids. They were their mother's daughters, burdened with her loss, with the love they bore for each other. What had first seemed a lesson in sibling affinity was beginning to appear more like a script from which they'd dared not stray. Kate had taught them this, demanded this, and, in Elin's opinion, it was no different than Elin demanding obedience from Fluke. In Kate's attempt to stop history from repeating itself she'd taken things too far. Come hell or high water, the compassion these girls felt for one another must be adhered to, good or bad, win or lose, unnatural in its force against their pain.

Quincy had sobbed into her hands.

Averlee was quick on her feet, leaping around Fluke to get to her sister, to save her from herself. "It's all right," she said, peeling Quincy's fingers from her eyes. "It's fine!"

Elin couldn't take another second. "Come," she said to Fluke, and he followed her outside into the blinding sun of the front porch, where Elin had spent much of the last three weeks melting in the heat, her skin darker than it had been in years. She had the urge to pick up the phone and scream at her sister for dying. How dare she leave them like this? What was Elin supposed to do with *two kids*? What should she teach them about fighting? About their mother being dead? About their *father*? "What the fuck?" she wanted to say, and then did say, loudly, above her head into the willows. She never wanted to be a mother. Had no instincts for it. In fact, the minute Quincy shoved Averlee down it was the goddamn Etch A Sketch all over again. She wanted to sling a dishtowel in their faces.

Sweat ran down the sides of her face, and yet she couldn't bring herself to go back inside and say the right thing. She did not know what the right thing was. Maybe it was leaving them alone to work it out. Maybe that was the direst decision she could make.

Every time she tried to imagine the future, the road supposed to lead them up and out of this mess, she could not picture what it should look like. A thick black curtain fell on her imagination. Her sister dying seemed like just the start, the beginning of worse things to come. Tragedy came in threes. Isn't that what her grandmother used to say? Mercy me. In threes. But from what point in time did the counting begin? How far back did Elin need to go?

That was all she could think about on the porch yesterday, and now here as she pulled herself out of bed, turned, and jostled Fluke's hip. He lifted his head, glanced at her, and lay back down. "You're a bad dog," she whispered. He closed his eyes.

Elin shuffled to the bathroom. Neal, assuming she could find him, and assuming he even wanted his daughters, well, what then? What the hell would that look like? Because what kind of father abandons his own children? It was a story she'd never gotten to the bottom of, never cared to know. What would Neal do if the law *made* him take Averlee and Quincy against his will?

Magnolia branches rasped against the shingles on the roof. Elin missed home. She missed the purple wisteria out her bedroom window and the neighbor's tabby and the hummingbird at the window. She missed Rudi, the man he was, the man she thought he was. She missed herself, the woman she'd pretended to be, a woman so much easier to be than this one dragging her feet across the floor.

She dressed quietly in shorts and a black tank top, the uniform of her days. She peeked into the next room, where the girls still slept, the furniture large and dark in the morning light, too heavy for the space it occupied, enclosing their tiny bodies in the bed, where their limbs flung outward, everywhere, as if broken ten different ways.

She crept downstairs with Fluke and then sat outside on the front porch steps while he sniffed around the yard. The grove next door was especially rich after a midnight rain, orange and peat, a trace of fruit rot, blackbirds hopping busily from soil to tree. Elin cradled her head down onto her knees. She had been in Florida for one month. Back in Portland the days would be cooling after an already mild summer, the leaves of white aspens in the hills taking on the first yellow tint of autumn.

"I want a divorce," she'd said when Rudi picked up the phone the morning after Kate died. It was the first time they had spoken, exactly one week and two days after she left.

"I can't exactly blame you," he said, with only a brief hesitation, as if she'd just told him she was grabbing takeout on the way home and he couldn't quite decide what he wanted. Would she have felt better if he'd burst into tears?

"My sister is dead," she said.

"What did you just say?"

"My nieces are here with me."

He gasped, and the drama of it, however genuine, annoyed her.

"I would appreciate a quick divorce. I trust you won't screw me over any more than you already have."

"*Elin . . .*"

"I just need to be out from under it."

"I don't know what to say. What a shock. . . . I'm so sorry."

There it was again, *soary*, like something you couldn't spell in the English language.

"I want the house," Elin said.

"You can have the house," he said, quick and generous, but of course the house was nothing compared to what his dealership was worth. He'd owned it for fifteen years and would still own it fifteen years from now, and none of that would be hers and she did not care.

"This is all very civilized," she said. "Thank you." Her gratitude was sincere but she didn't say this. She didn't tell him she appreciated that he was, and always had been, kind to her. A kind and considerate liar.

"Takes one to know one," Kate said in Elin's mind. Said with laughter, cracking herself up inside Elin's head. Elin dripped sweat onto the porch.

"You can leave me alone now," Elin said, watching Fluke run laps around the yard. "Go off and be dead." She didn't mean that. Christ. She didn't mean that at all.

She stood and whistled sharply for Fluke and they headed inside so she could be there when the girls woke, to help them dress and get downstairs to Shug's overstuffed breakfast that had not failed to make their eyes bug. And Shug would not fail to make them smile, and Elin would not fail to take her migraine medication with an eight-ounce glass of water, but she would certainly fail these children in a multitude of ways by the time they crawled back into their beds that night, their trust in her crowded out by their justified doubt and suspicion.

THIRTY-TWO

VIVVIE HAD STRUGGLED TO KEEP Big Boy calm under the icy hose that day, his legs shifting side to side, slick and quivering, a wily, furry bulk wrangling through her arms and through her tears. He was whining, whimpering with terror, a good dog wanting to do the good thing, but he was no more capable of erasing what he'd just seen than she was.

A movement above Vivvie's shoulder caught her eye. Elin, peering down from the bathroom window. Vivvie shoved the dog against the siding and wiped her eyes in the crook of her arm, but she knew full well it was too late, and she kept her arm to her face for crying, the hose running down her leg into her shoe.

What conclusion could a child that young come to? As a teenager Elin had alluded to what she'd seen that day, her words laced with menace. Of course everything she said as a teenager was laced with menace, with complaint, a constant judgment against Vivvie, but it was clear then as now that the only daughter Vivvie had left in this world was plagued by misery, by a rattling demon that Vivvie herself had infected her with the day Elin saw her through the bathroom window.

Vivvie felt the phantom sting of brushwood tearing the skin off her back, the scent of autumn soil beneath her fingernails from clawing and scrambling for the rifle behind her. It was late morning but if it hadn't been for Wink honking his horn—a signal meant to get her attention—she might have left the kitchen and gone back to bed, mired in the same thoughts that had kept her awake most of the night. She peered out above the sink.

Wink had dropped the tailgate on his truck, stepped back, and stared into the bed with crossed arms.

"What's in there?" Vivvie yelled through the screen.

"A Ping-Pong table," he answered without looking in her direction.

"A Ping-Pong table."

"Yes, ma'am. A Ping-Pong table. From the flea market."

"Why?" she asked, but she had a feeling.

"Why not?"

Vivvie went outside and joined him behind his truck.

"Where are you going to put a Ping-Pong table?" she asked.

"Right out under these trees. The sun won't fade it in the shade, and the rain won't get at it too hard." He pointed near the bull's-eye still taped to the tree, its rings pink, bled nearly clear from the rain.

"The legs will sink into the sand," Vivvie said. "It'll be lopsided."

Wink studied the yard.

Vivvie turned to her driveway and sighed. "You could put it over there at the top of my driveway in the shade. There's plenty of room for me to park the truck closer to the street."

"The sun'll eat the paint off your truck."

They stared at the dull, salt-eaten hood of the truck. Wink laughed, and then Vivvie did, too, just a little, and for the first time in weeks.

"My granddaughters might enjoy it," she said, soberly.

"Well. You sure?"

"I'm sure."

Wink scratched the palm of his hand.

"You still got splinters?"

"Nah."

"You ever finish that whistle?"

Wink nodded. "I painted it red. It's all set for trying someone's nerves."

Vivvie smiled, glanced again at the driveway.

"How's she doing?" he asked. "Elin. With your granddaughters."

Vivvie waved a hand as if at a fly. "She claims she's got everything under control. She's lying."

"I see."

"But I don't think it would be fair for them to stay here with me either. I'm not young anymore. Far from it."

"You're only what, fifty?"

"You write your own stuff or hire someone on the side?"

"You walked right into it."

"You want me to help you pull that thing on out of your truck?"

"How's your back?" he asked.

"How's yours?"

"Well, it was fine until the day I pulled this Ping-Pong table out of my truck."

"And your neighbor dropped it on your foot," she said, expecting a grin and could see it had started, but then he stopped and looked directly at her.

"I'm sorry for what you're going through, Vivvie. I don't know what else to say."

She couldn't look him in the eye. "You've said all that needs saying," she started, but before she could finish he was holding her in his arms. She was holding him, too.

"Why do you always smell like salty popcorn?" she asked, her cheek against his chest, eyelids closed, red against the sun. The red shirt in the tree, red all over the dog—

"I didn't know I smelled like popcorn."

"Yes," she said. "You do."

"With butter?"

"No."

Wink had helped Vivvie and the movers Elin hired pack up Kate's house, get the furniture and kitchenware, along with Kate's clothes and books, into a storage unit and then stuff the girls' toys, books, and clothes, as well as Kate's notebooks and personal papers, into Vivvie's spare room. When Kate's house was finally bare, Vivvie had stood at the open door looking in at the nothingness, at what no longer was, a bright light of life extinguished. Gone this cocoon of an unmarred life, a mother and her children so happy in the face of inevitable doom. A tarnished old shame, like metal, like the taste of blood, filled Vivvie's tongue. She winced, and winced again as Wink swept the front room with such warmhearted care, the crosswind carrying his popcorn smell toward her until she could no longer bear it and walked away.

She stepped back from him now, embarrassed, distrustful of her emotions.

"Well," he said.

"Well."

They latched onto the lip of the table and wedged it halfway out. A leg unfolded to the ground near Vivvie's foot. She peered underneath.

"It's only got three legs," she said.

"I know."

"What good is a three-legged Ping-Pong table?"

"It's solid wood. They don't make them like this anymore. All I have to do is nail a two-by-four under there. I already got one here in the truck. Besides, the woman was nearly giving this thing away."

"I can't imagine."

"It was a steal," Wink said, and Vivvie didn't stop nodding until she got into her truck and backed it down her driveway.

After that she and Wink heaved the Ping-Pong table free and toted it into the driveway's shade. Vivvie stepped back. The strangeness of it, like a beached whale at which Vivvie could not help but stare. The view of the yard, the woods beyond it opening up after being blocked for decades by Jackson's truck.

Wink wedged the two-by-four underneath. "I'll fasten it in a minute," he said, and wiped his hands on his pants. He glanced at Vivvie.

"You sure about this?" He scratched his chin. "We can always put it somewhere else."

"You want to put it somewhere else?"

"No. No I don't. Right here is fine."

"I think Elin is keeping them away from me," Vivvie said, as unexpectedly as a Ping-Pong table arriving in the driveway.

"Your granddaughters?"

"She doesn't want me to see them. She hasn't said so, but she keeps making excuses, like they have appointments or they're in the middle of dinner or reading a book or whatever else she can come up with every time I call. 'They're trying to recover,' she keeps saying."

"But they would be, wouldn't they?"

"I guess. Sure. But that's not my point."

The conversation had nowhere to go. What she didn't say was that she feared an ugly pattern coming over her right after Kate died. Vivvie had pulled away from her granddaughters, the hurt in their eyes too familiar, the past too close to her skin. She'd taken a step back, filled the hours by following the paper trail of Kate's life, phone calls and errands, anything that would force her out of the same room as her granddaughters. As her daughter.

"I'm sorry," she said. "I shouldn't have started in on that."

"No need to apologize."

"Yeah, there is."

Wink pulled two paddles from his back pocket and a small white ball from his front. "Let's see what you got," he said.

"I don't think so."

"Come on. Be a sport."

Vivvie hesitated, could hear the phone ringing in the kitchen through the open window, but the thought of answering exhausted her whole body. She did not want to listen to the news on the other end.

Wink tipped his head toward the table. "Two out of three. Loser makes lunch."

THIRTY-THREE

AIRPORT SECURITY HAD THE FEEL of a much larger inspection, a deeper examination of Neal's trustworthiness, of seeing what he, quite literally, had up his sleeve. Profuse sweating was the first sign of a liar, of someone with something to hide. Was he a man with corrupt intentions? A TSA agent asked him to step to the side while he felt up and down Neal's legs, back, and underarms with rubber-gloved hands. A wand was drawn over every inch of his body and Neal could not help but feel the man would find something, a pocketknife, a box cutter he never used but had somehow placed in his jeans by mistake. When the agent finally released him with a wave toward the gates and a look of regret that said he knew that Neal was hiding something, was getting away with that which he did not deserve, Neal nodded as if in agreement. "Thank you," he said, and fumbled into his shoes.

He was two hours early and found a quiet corner to cool down and pull out his cell phone. Someone ought to be aware that he was on his way. He didn't know where to find his daughters. He called his cousin but she didn't know anything, and why would she?

Vivvie wasn't answering her phone.

He didn't know how to find Elin. He wasn't sure he was ready to start looking. Since getting the mail yesterday things had been coming to him in doses. It seemed that under the circumstances he would quite naturally be confused or numb. He ought to be in shock. But as he made his way to the gate, and then sat down by the giant glass windows and waited to board, he did not feel any of those things. It was like being caught in a warm trance. A quiet, sun-drenched man in a rust-colored airport, his head filling with visions of his daughters in need—tiny little things asking after him for years, the hardship caused by his absence, the despair of Kate's decline. He had not been there, he had not been anywhere at all, and he pressed his fingers into his eyes to still the weeping.

Maybe the weeping was the shock.

He was flying first class. He'd never flown first class but it was all that was available on short notice, and now he felt uneasy at the thought of being fussed over. He did not want the attention. He needed to process all the ways in which Kate had lied to him, her elaborate scheme woven over a long period of time. He needed to process the overriding anger that surged through him at intervals, zapping like a Taser throughout the night. He had been such a self-loathing idiot, buying into everything she accused him of without question. "You are ruining me," she'd said, "ruining your own children. I have never been more miserable in my life than I am here with you, and in turn you are denying your own daughters the mother they deserve, the one I'm trying so hard to be." Then she'd used his feelings for her sister against him, a truth he could not deny, her words tearing him apart like a serrated knife, scattering him into so many pieces across the country that it had been impossible to make a full repair. All these years later he still felt like Frankenstein, half monster, half man, now sitting in a clamoring crowd, hand covering his eyes, forcing himself to appear as if he were normal. He feared he just might blurt the whole story to the first person who showed him the smallest kindness.

The plane was starting to board when Vivvie finally answered her phone.

THIRTY-FOUR

ELIN DECIDED THAT TALKING WHILE driving was easier. She didn't have to look her nieces in the eye, and they didn't have to look at her. They could say what they wanted to say. She could do the same.

"But where did she go?" Quincy asked for what felt like the hundredth time.

"I don't know," Elin answered. "Heaven, I guess. I hope. I don't know."

"But why can't I talk to her?"

"Because she's gone."

"Can't you ask her to come back?"

"Quincy," Averlee said. "Stop."

Elin glanced in her mirror. Averlee shook her head at the window. Quincy stared into her lap.

"Let's get some lunch," Elin said. "I'm hungry. Aren't you two hungry?"

They stopped at the Brandywine Sandwich Shoppe on Park Avenue. Elin wasn't hungry, and from the looks of things, neither were her nieces. But who cared? They could get up and walk away from grilled cheese sandwiches and cookies if they felt like it. They could stroll the sidewalks and shop all day, too. They could stay in bed and watch TV and eat candy for breakfast. There were no rules, no routines, no blueprints for how this was supposed to go, and anyway, it just didn't seem to *matter*.

Her mother's days were different. As executor of Kate's will—an odd fact that had Elin wondering if Kate had foreseen how such a responsibility would take over their mother's life with goals and lists, have her marching toward every challenge, a new problem with every new day as a way of keeping her busy. The electric company refused to shut off the power without a signature from Kate. The credit union where Kate's accounts were held was perplexed over what a power of attorney actually allowed when it came to Kate's money. Same with the credit card companies. Everyone wanted something her mother couldn't get, or had yet to get. There was always more for her to do. Answers and signatures, and where was the father of the children? Elin could hear the complicated weariness in her mother's voice on the phone, but she could hear an arrogance, too, a pride of ownership for the messy occupation that was hers and hers alone.

Elin made excuses. A flicker of panic rose every time her mother asked to see Averlee and Quincy, which wasn't as often as one would expect. Over the last couple of weeks her mother went from hands-on caring to nearly vanishing after Kate's death. It was too familiar. Grief ought to be debilitating, ought to bring the living, the loved, together in their sorrow. For Elin, to talk to her nieces meant taking their hand, to leave them alone in a room meant she had to first touch a shoulder, the top of a head, a knee. If her mother had cried Elin didn't see it, and the only hugs she gave the girls appeared stiff and brief, a quick pat on the back at the door. Old habits die hard, emotional triggers like stubborn weeds, profoundly twisted and entrenched, rising to the surface. Elin's own insides knotted every time she heard her mother's voice, every time her mother averted her eyes from those two little girls.

They picked at their food in silence.

Averlee held her blue water bottle to the window, and the sun shone through the curve of the glass. "We can wash the label off and put it in the kitchen window. We can put some of Mrs. Pearl's flowers in it."

Elin felt her eyes go wide. She struggled to keep a straight face. Did Averlee believe they would return to the house they'd been living in? Of course she did. Elin hadn't told her any different. What had she told them? "It's like a short vacation at the pretty B and B. You'll see. It'll be nice." She did not know how to be straight with children or if being straight with children was what one needed to be.

"Where do you live again?" Averlee asked.

"Oregon."

"Where's that?"

"I need to show you on a map so you'll remember. It's on the west coast of the United States. Right above California."

Averlee studied her blue bottle in the sun.

"Have you two ever been there?" Elin asked.

Each shook her head.

"What about California?"

"Our mom took us to Melbourne Beach once," Quincy said.

"We've never been out of the state," Averlee said. "What do you do in Oregon?"

"I work. A lot."

"Do you have a husband?" Quincy asked.

Elin cupped her left hand inside her right, massaging her finger where the ring used to be. "I did. I do. I won't for much longer."

The girls glanced at one another.

"You did or you do?" Averlee asked.

"How about we head across the street and check out the bookstore?" Elin said.

"What's your husband's name?" Averlee asked.

"Rudi. Rudiger."

"Weird," Quincy said.

"Yeah. It is. What do you say we go now?"

"Our dad's name is Neal," Quincy said.

Elin stopped. "I know."

"Do you know him?"

"Yes," Elin said. "Do *you*?"

"No," they answered together.

"How do you know him?" Averlee asked.

"We used to be friends, a long time ago."

"And now you're not?" Quincy said.

"Oh, I suppose we are. With him being your dad that certainly makes him a friend of mine, don't you think?"

"Will he come down from the mountain now?" Quincy asked.

"What mountain?"

"Our mom told us he was mountain climbing and it was really big and would take a long time to come down."

"Mountain climbing? What *mountain*?"

Averlee shrugged.

"Do you think he would come down if we sent him a letter about our mom?" Quincy asked.

"Who would take a letter up a mountain?" Averlee asked her.

"He might." Elin stood. "Let's head across the street. I'm tired of sitting."

They gathered their books and pencils off the table, finished a glass of juice, used the bathroom, and tied a shoe before they were finally out the door. It was exhausting to watch and wrangle. She did not understand how mothers did this all day, every day.

The bookstore smelled of old paper and ink and coffee. It was a large, single room with mahogany bookshelves and a waxy red concrete floor. A collection of art and design books on a center table immediately caught Elin's eye. As did a hefty collection on the works by Louis Comfort Tiffany. She flipped through the pages.

The woman behind the counter wore a sleek jade blouse, a black skirt, and black heels, attire more suited to working at an art gallery than a bookstore. She approached Elin, told her that not only was the book a beautiful collection of glass in pictures, but the Charles Hosmer Morse Museum of American Art was just up the street, holding the largest real collection of Tiffany glass in the world.

She had forgotten. Or at least put it out of her mind. Her mother had taken her and Kate when they were young. The visit was really for Elin, for her interest in color and art. Kate had done nothing but complain.

"Are you just visiting?" the woman asked.

Elin set the book down. A chill ran through her shoulders and she shivered. "Yes," she said.

"Have you girls been to Disney World?" the woman asked.

Good question. Elin had no idea, and not being privy to this information caused a sudden jerk in the back of her throat. This was a conversation she would never have with her sister, would have never had *anyway* if she'd lived, and this thought was becoming as difficult to manage as the fact that her sister was dead.

Averlee shook her head no. Of course Kate had never taken them there. But could she have even if she'd wanted to? Probably not. She lived like a monk. They didn't even have a TV, and the computer given to her by "the center" was at least twelve years old.

"We've got plans for Disney," Elin said, and her nieces stared at her with puckered, puzzled expressions as she ushered them toward the children's books along the back wall. An hour later Elin had purchased five hundred dollars' worth of a children's library. An investment in them, she told herself. A contribution toward their future.

THIRTY-FIVE

"IT'S NEAL RHODES," HE'D SAID.

Vivvie nearly dropped the phone. She'd just come in from playing Ping-Pong, her cheeks warmly flushed, her mind out of sorts, emotions like birds taking flight in too many directions. And here was Wink across the room with a glass of water, his back to her, swallowing, pretending not to listen.

"I'm on my way into town," Neal said. "I'm so sorry about Kate."

Whatever he said after that didn't stick, and Vivvie hung up, walked into the spare room, and sat in the middle of the floor. Three weeks ago she'd cleaned this room for the girls, already thinking of the space as theirs, of getting a second bed and buying colorful drapes and linens, of making it feel like a girl's room, and now it was in worse shape than before—boxes lining walls, stacked on the bed, and blocking the closet door. Worse still was the fact that when she did finally get it cleaned out it might very well be because she was sending every bit of it with Neal.

Wink stood in the doorway. Vivvie wasn't sure for how long.

"He's coming for his daughters," she said.

"I kind of gathered that from your call. You went white in the face." He sat across from her on the floor. "What did he say?"

"Only that he was coming. Least that's all I heard. He said we'd talk more when he got here."

"I know it's none of my business. But what did Kate intend for them? I mean, she must have planned something. Did she leave a will?"

Vivvie nodded, said nothing, and then stood and began ripping open a box. "She wanted Elin to have her daughters," she said. "I haven't told her. I haven't told anyone. It's in her will. They and everything she owned were supposed to go to her sister."

Vivvie leaned forward, rested her head on her arm, and breathed. She could feel Wink moving behind her, and then his hand on her back.

"That didn't really take into account that they still had a father," he said.

"No. It did not."

"I'm no lawyer but it seems to me that a living parent overrides the wishes of a will."

"It does. It will."

"Why haven't you told Elin?"

It wasn't until the words were fully formed that Vivvie realized they were true. "I don't think she wants them. She doesn't want them. And she doesn't want me to have them either."

Wink rubbed a circle at the center of her back. Vivvie closed her eyes. He let go a loud, heavy sigh. "What's in the box?" he asked.

"Kate's notebooks."

"Like journals or something?"

"Could be. She used to write poems and stuff like that. I have no idea what's written here. I didn't want to know. But now I do. Maybe there's stuff about Neal."

"Incriminating stuff?"

Vivvie shrugged.

Wink dropped his hand. "I can leave you alone—"

Vivvie faced him, so close she could see the elaborate, cross-stitched lines at the corners of his eyes, the grey stubble on his chin.

She could see his eyes were more grey than blue. "Stay," she said. "If you don't mind."

"I don't mind at all." He reached around her and lifted the box. "Where do you want it?"

Vivvie studied the room. The only free space was where they stood, a pocket of air in a cave. "Right here is just fine."

They sat cross-legged, facing one another, the box between them as Vivvie began removing the notebooks and asked Wink to do the same. He found a small box at the bottom, filled with what they quickly understood were Neal's letters to Averlee and Quincy. They'd never been opened. So they read those first, out loud to each other, page after page as tender as any poem.

THIRTY-SIX

ELIN DIDN'T BELIEVE IN GHOSTS or spirits, but a knock on the door of her room at the B and B sent Fluke into a barking, snarling frenzy, the likes of which she'd never seen, and when Elin jumped to her feet and demanded he stop, he would not back down. And this, more than anything, frightened her—how hard it was for him to restrain himself, as if he knew more than she did, as if he sensed something beyond the knuckles on the door.

Elin clapped her hands in his face and finally he sat back and licked the stiff hairs around his mouth, his front legs shivering with tension. "Stay," she said, and he did what he was told.

No ghosts, no spirits, only Shug handing Elin a piece of stationery with decorative paisley trim through the crack in the door. "I'm so sorry about Fluke," Elin said, afraid to open it all the way, afraid he might bite now, too. "He's never done this. He's always so well behaved."

"Oh, sweetheart. Don't apologize. He's been through so much. You all have. He's just a dog. Not nearly as good at hiding his emotions."

And what was that supposed to mean? Elin looked down at the stationery in her hands.

"Your mother called," Shug said.

This was written on the paper.

"She said you weren't answering your cell phone," Shug said.

This was written there, too. As was, *Call me. He's on his way.*

"She said you'd know what it means."

At the bottom was written one more line: *There's something I haven't told you about the will.*

THIRTY-SEVEN

ELIN DECIDED IT WASN'T A good idea to deliver the news before bed so she waited until morning and then woke the girls extra early by pulling back the drapes, the wooden curtain rings clacking all the way down the wooden rod, and after the racket came the sharp, blinding sun in their eyes.

Before today she'd let them sleep as long as they wished, and here she was on the bed next to Quincy. They pulled away from her, raw nerves and frightened, suspicious eyes. "It's all right," Elin said, feeling differently toward them, more protective, more responsible, more watchful of her own behavior after the puzzling news her mother had shared with her about the will. "We've got a visitor coming. You need to get dressed, brush your hair, and hurry up for breakfast."

"Who is it?" Averlee asked, bolting upright against her pillows.

Quincy was still trying to sit up.

"Your father," Elin said, and their heads shot up as if by the physical force of her words.

"He came off the mountain?" Quincy asked.

"Apparently," Elin said.

Averlee appeared terrified.

"It's all right," Elin said, patting Averlee's knee. "Shug is making breakfast a little early for you. We've got a big day ahead of us. It's going to be fine."

As if on cue the smell of bacon drifted up the stairs and into the room.

"Pick out something you like to wear. Something comfortable."

"Is he taking us?" Averlee said.

"Oh. No, Averlee. He's just coming to see you." Elin averted her eyes, looking around the room. Maybe he *could* take them and there wasn't a thing she could do. Maybe that was the truth. Temporary custody was just that, *temporary*, until a better solution was found.

In the dining room the early sun cast different shadows than it did later in the morning, making the room, the mood, stranger than it already was. Everyone ate their pancakes in silence. Even Shug, whose friendly, energetic nature never failed to infuse whole rooms, was subdued. She cleared the table and repeatedly wiped her hands down her apron.

Averlee pushed her half-eaten pancake away. "I'm full," she said, dressed in her old shorts and T-shirt.

Quincy was still eating. Elin had never seen her eat so much. The excitement buzzed off her skin. She was wearing the outfit Elin had bought her, white cotton with a pink, crew neck collar, brown leather sandals that still crunched with newness when she walked.

"Why don't you head upstairs and brush your teeth?" Elin said to Averlee. "I'll wait here until your sister is finished."

Averlee hesitated. They'd always gone up together after every meal.

"It's all right. Take Fluke with you. Go on, boy, follow Averlee." Elin pointed and Fluke stood at Averlee's feet, and Elin understood that the anticipation of seeing her father was making the loss of her mother all the more real. Such a monumental moment, and who else would she want to tell but her mother?

Elin took Averlee's hand inside both of hers. "It'll be okay," she said. "It will."

Averlee gently pulled away.

Half an hour later the three of them waited on the front-porch bench. Neal had called and left a message with Shug that he'd be there at ten o'clock. It was nine forty-five.

Elin fanned her hair off the back of her neck. It didn't seem that hot, not yet, but sweat was a viscous oil coating her nape and she caught herself sighing repeatedly, forced herself to stop. She was dressed in capris instead of shorts, and her white blouse instead of the tank top that would have kept her slightly cooler. She fanned and fidgeted with nervous anticipation. All three of their lives were about to be altered in ways Elin wouldn't allow herself to imagine. Change was the only certainty.

Quincy swung her legs beneath the bench and strained to see up the street. Averlee looked as if she were traveling alone on a bus, staring off to the side, hands in her lap, her face a study in the forsaken. More than once Elin had to stop herself from promising that they wouldn't have to leave with him, that he wasn't coming to take them away.

A tan sedan appeared in the distance. It drove slowly down the street, and then paused at the driveway before turning in.

Elin wiped her palms on her thighs. She cleared her throat, and flashed a forced smile down onto Averlee and Quincy as she stood.

It felt like a full five minutes before the car door opened and he stepped out, a man in aviator sunglasses, a black T-shirt and jeans, leather shoes, blond hair in waves around his ears.

Son of a bitch, she thought, and may have even said it. She looked at the girls, then Neal, then the girls, and finally only at Neal.

Quincy stood and grabbed Elin's hand.

Neal touched his heart and Elin did the same before quickly shoving her hand in her pocket. He removed his sunglasses and rubbed his eyes. He put the glasses back on, opened the rear car door, and pulled out a suitcase.

"What's that?" Elin said.

He closed the door and began walking toward them. "A suitcase."

"What are you doing with it?"

He stopped nearly ten feet from the porch and removed his sunglasses again. His tan skin had aged around the eyes and mouth, thin lines that did not detract in any way from his looks, at least not from there. "Wow," he whispered, and let go of the suitcase and opened his arms. Quincy rushed toward him. He kneeled and held her against him, eyes clenched in a bliss that Elin could not bear to see.

Averlee looked up at her, sighed, and slowly walked toward Neal. "Sweetheart," he said. "Do you remember me?" He embraced both girls at once.

Elin crossed her arms and looked off into the grove. She wished she could go inside the house but what if the girls turned around and she wasn't there? Would they think she'd abandoned them? Would they even care? She did not want to see that they didn't care.

Neal let go and stood, smiling so hard he laughed. "Wow," he said. "Just wow."

"What are you doing with the suitcase?" Elin asked.

His smile grew faint when he looked up at her. "Checking in," he said.

THIRTY-EIGHT

LAST NIGHT VIVVIE AND WINK had begun reading Kate's oldest note-books first. Neither of them knew much about poetry but both agreed that as the years progressed so had Kate's writing, even as her penmanship began to fail. There were pages of scraps, too, words in margins, phrases that made no sense. *A freckled hand, frosted lips, west wind, broken feather, angry eel.* The word *mother* appeared often, sometimes circled, sometimes in a square, often by itself, and Vivvie had no way of knowing if Kate had been thinking of herself or Vivvie or of some consummate mother who lived exclusively inside Kate's own head.

Kate wrote about yellow birds and waxy plants, about twisty trees and daughters beneath the leaves. She wrote about busted hearts and the pleasures of sex, until finally, just before midnight, Vivvie and Wink discovered poems she had written about death, about endings, about the heartache of leaving others behind.

"I think that's enough for one day," Vivvie had said. "Maybe we can go through more over breakfast."

"My place or yours?" he asked with a smirk.

"Mine. You already made lunch today. I'll make you breakfast."

"I had to make lunch. You won fair and square. I owed you."

"You've been a big help around here. I owe you, too."

"The pleasure's mine," he said, and she walked him to the door, watched him disappear into the yard, listened for the ache of screen door hinges, and then the close of the front door after that. She watched until the light came on in his kitchen, and from the cover of dark, she watched until the light disappeared and there was nothing but night sounds, frogs and crickets, her company for years, and still she did not want to go back inside.

Now here they were, the morning after what had felt like a date, finishing their eggs and biscuits at Vivvie's kitchen table, the mood as intimate and awkward as if they'd spent the night together. They drank their coffee in silence, smiling every now and then above their mugs.

"It's kind of stuffy in that back room," Vivvie said. "How about we lug what's left out here to the table?"

And so they did, still smiling meekly as they crossed into each other's space, clearing the dishes, settling back into their chairs.

Half an hour later, while lost inside a poem about icy cold springs and a daughter's wet curls, Vivvie was jerked back into the room by a feeling, as if the sun had been extinguished, and with it, every living thing on earth. She raised her eyes. Wink's jaw had fallen open, his hand cupping his chin and cheek, eyes rounded on the notebook where his other hand lay at the top of the page.

She knew before she asked. Knew it like he'd said it, like he'd pointed a finger and accused her, sick with understanding, outraged in disbelief.

What in God's name had she been thinking, allowing him to snoop through the personal writings of her daughter?

Wink swallowed. His eyes rolled up to meet hers.

"Go ahead," Vivvie said. "Tell me."

He turned the notebook around and slid it across the table.

A poem called "On the Night She Killed My Father." The first two lines read:

On the night she killed my father
She made casualties of us all.

Vivvie snapped the notebook shut, shoved her chair back, and turned her back to the table. She held her head between her knees. No need to read the rest. She already knew what was written there.

She felt Wink rise from his chair. "Don't," Vivvie said, her insides shattering, sharp and loud as glass. "Please. Just leave me be."

He was next to her now, touching her shoulder. She jerked away. But a wail sprung, a series of retched cries broke free. *Make it stop*, she thought, *make it stop. Stop. Stop.* But it would not. It gained in strength, a torrent of sobs drowning out the room. This was not about what she'd done to Jackson, not about being sorry for that. This was grief, plain and simple, long in the coming, a greedy, wretched sorrow laying her to waste. Vivvie wailed, recalling a sympathy card like it was yesterday: *A voice is heard in Ramah, mourning and great weeping, Rachel weeping for her children and refusing to be comforted, because they are no more.* But it was from years ago, when a coworker's son died in a car accident, and someone had printed that verse right on the front, and here and now Vivvie wailed, thinking of how they had passed those cards out at the door, the cruelty of it, a grieving mother reading that merciless truth, passed around again and again in the light of day for all the world to see.

When she began to calm, Wink touched her and this time she didn't move. He sat beside her, laid his arm full across her shoulders.

"No," she cried, shaking her head. "Go away." The thought came to her that maybe she could reverse what had happened, that there was still a window of opportunity to shift time and place, say or do the right thing. She had not done the right thing, but maybe now she would, even as she did not know what it was, even as her mind was telling her that these thoughts made no sense, the same mind that carried through with the hope, the belief that she could overthrow what had happened, and put it in reverse.

"Vivvie. If you didn't want me to leave last night you sure as hell don't want me to leave now."

"Yes, I do," she said.

Wink pulled slightly away. "Come on, now," he said. "She's a poet. That's just a figure of speech."

Vivvie wailed again. It took her breath. She shook her head repeatedly, until finally, sucking at the air, she muttered, "No. No. No. No. *No.*"

Wink rubbed her back. "But you're not saying . . . Are you saying?"

Vivvie began to nod.

"No. You're not saying . . . Wait a minute." His hand was gone from her now. "Did you really *kill* their father?"

Vivvie sat upright, gripped her hair at the roots, and squeezed her eyes shut. "Yes." She opened her eyes, felt the dullness of her stare, her reptile face.

Wink appeared confused, as if still trying to gauge the truth of her answer. "That can't be right."

"But it is."

"You shot him?" he asked.

"Yes."

"With a rifle?"

"Yes."

"And killed him?"

Vivvie tilted her head back, closed her eyes, and dropped her arms with a sigh.

"All right then," Wink said. "All right. Well. We're just going to, you know, I don't know what to say."

"I told you to leave."

"I know you did."

Vivvie opened her eyes, turned, and glanced at the notebook.

"This is bad, Vivvie. I mean, *you*, the way you're feeling right now. I think I should call someone. I don't think you're going to be all right."

She laughed and wiped her cheeks. "Who are you going to call? The game warden?"

It wasn't funny. But in the silence that followed Vivvie began to feel light-headed, as if a ten-pound tumor had been cut from her skull.

"Can I ask you something?" Wink said.

She didn't say yes, she didn't say no.

"Why did you do it?"

"I loved him."

Wink was silent.

"He was suffering," she said, and Wink nodded once.

"It was passed down. That's what happened here. What's taken half of my family."

"Oh, Lord. Vivvie."

"His was much worse. It was so quick."

The phone rang but Vivvie didn't look up.

Wink stroked her back, the only sound in the room her muffled, sporadic sobs. "I don't know that it helps you to hear this," Wink said. "But my wife was in a world of pain, and then completely lost to a morphine drip before the cancer finally took her."

Vivvie stopped abruptly. "I'm sorry. I didn't know." His wife died shortly after Wink moved with her next door. The first time Vivvie had a full conversation with Wink was when she brought him a macaroni casserole and cornbread and asked if there was anything she could do. He'd told her no, and they talked about the yard, how he would like to care for all of it, his and hers.

"Can I ask you another question?" Wink said.

"That's already a question," Vivvie said.

He smiled sadly, and then his face turned hard and serious. "How come you never got caught?"

Vivvie wiped her nose on the back of her hand, thought of Quincy, and fell into a mix of laughter and tears. Wink handed her a paper towel from the sink. "It looked like a hunting accident," she said.

Wink glanced around the room, for what, Vivvie couldn't tell. The gun? A witness? The door? "And they never suspected you?"

"Maybe. Nothing ever came of it if they did."

"But your daughters knew. Kate knew."

"*Elin* knew. She must have told Kate."

"Did Elin *see it happen*?"

Vivvie shook her head. "No. But she knew."

Wink was quiet for too long.

"Are you going to the police with this?" Vivvie asked. "Because if you are I've got to say I don't care anymore."

Wink reached for her hand, and she let him have it, hers as hot and damp as his. He leaned forward and held her shoulder, pulling her close.

"No, Vivvie. I'm not going to tell another living soul."

She nodded, her lips twisting against her will, his kindness causing more stinging in her chest.

"I'm sorry," he said. "I'm sorry you've had to carry this, all of this, by yourself. Lord, what you're made of, Vivvie." He gathered her to his shoulder and held her there until she stopped crying, until the light had shifted significantly, and the day felt like a different day from the one they'd began. A hazy, dreamy day where nothing else was expected of them, and she said, "All right now. That's enough. My ass is falling asleep."

THIRTY-NINE

ELIN HAD CARRIED HER LAPTOP out to the porch with the intention of getting caught up on emails, of seeing what and how she might reshape, might feasibly reassemble, however small, a working life, any life.

Neal and the girls were still inside eating strawberry ice cream, courtesy of Shug. When Quincy dribbled half a spoonful down her chin, Neal had dabbed it with a napkin, and Elin pushed her chair from the table. "I'll be out front if anyone needs me," she said, but no one gave a sign that they might.

Thirty minutes later Neal sat next to her on the bench. He looked off into the yard, and then the grove next door as if he didn't know her, as if they were strangers in a park.

"Where are the girls?" Elin asked.

"Inside, with Shug. I told them I needed to talk to you alone."

"Oh. This should be interesting."

Neal didn't smile.

"Kate told them you were mountain climbing all these years," Elin said. "What was that all about?"

"They asked me about it, too. I just made something up on the spot. I don't know what Kate was thinking. I never knew what she'd told them. Maybe it was the best explanation she could think of."

"And what's yours? I mean, the real reason you left your kids behind?"

Neal rested his elbows onto the back of the bench. It brought him closer. He smelled of citrusy cologne. "You mean what did I tell myself in order to sleep at night?"

"That's not what I said."

"Isn't it?"

Elin raised an eyebrow. "Actually it *is*. What the fuck, Neal."

"You have no idea how complicated this whole thing is."

"You're joking, right?"

"I mean before. Everything from years before."

"You got me there." Elin crossed her arms. "And to be honest, I don't want to know."

"Kate could be very convincing."

Elin held up her palm. "I don't want to hear the details of your relationship with my sister."

"That's not what I'm getting at."

"I don't want to hear you blaming her for the fact that you left either."

"That's not what I'm doing, Elin, but it sure is nice to see you defending her. My how times have changed."

Elin slowly shook her head. "Nice shot."

"Look. You asked me a question. I'm doing my best to answer."

"Well, clearly you've got a long way to go."

Neal stood. "Maybe this isn't a good time."

"It's as good as any. Please. Sit down. I'll let you finish. I'd just as soon get it over with."

He lowered himself to the bench, and a minute later, said, "You never knew, I don't think you ever saw, this way Kate had—just hear me out. You never saw that part of her in the same way she never saw it in you. The two of you were so much alike."

Elin tossed her head back on the verge of laughter.

"I'm serious. I should know. Don't you think if anyone would know how alike you are it'd be me?"

"Nice how we were so interchangeable for you, Neal. Were you always this crass?"

"That is *not* what I meant. I'm not trying to be crass. It's the truth about her, and you, whether you care to see it or not."

"What is your point?"

"I trusted her in the same way I trusted you."

"Oh. Don't turn this on me. You were telling me about abandoning your children, remember?"

Neal pulled in a long breath. "Yes. I was. I am. And you're part of it, Elin. You're part of the whole goddamn thing."

"And how is that?"

"What I'm saying is Kate convinced me that I didn't deserve to have Averlee and Quincy in my life. She had me believing—well, keep in mind that I was *willing* to believe and I'll get to that in a minute—but what she claimed was that my presence demeaned her. That I was robbing her of the ability to be a good mother, and in turn robbing the girls of the happy, healthy mother they deserved. She was adamant about not being the kind of mother your own mother was. And it made sense to me. At the time it did."

"How did you *demean* her?"

Neal glanced at the porch and shook his head. "You need to understand I've spent my whole adult life trained to be aware of my surroundings, to know where I am, and avoid hazards at all costs."

"Are you comparing Kate to a burning house?"

He didn't answer.

"I don't get it. Was she making something up just to get rid of you? Or was whatever you did really that bad?"

"The whole thing was bad. Start to finish. An IDLS situation if there ever was one." This had been a running joke between them, an acronym used at the fire department for an "immediately dangerous to life or health" situation. "I see now what it really was, knowing what I know about her illness."

The trees gave them both something to look at. Neal's hands curled into fists near his knees. He continued. "But I had no idea back then that she clearly wanted the kids to herself. She didn't want me coming around on weekends and taking them away, not with so little time left in her life. And she had to have been afraid that I would take them completely away from her as soon as she was too sick to care for them. That I would insist on it and no court in the world would deny me. It was so damn selfish of her, and yet, I can't blame her, not now. How can I blame her? I'm here, and our daughters have got their whole lives ahead of them. And—"

Our daughters. Elin flinched. "What does any of this have to do with me? Why did you say I was part of it?"

"I never stopped loving you."

"Oh, for Christ's sake."

"You asked."

"Yeah, but come on. That's not even true."

Neal didn't look at her now.

"It's not," she said.

"Don't you ever get tired of hurting me?" he asked.

"No."

He met her eyes and Elin bit her lip to keep from laughing at her own cruelty, but it was too late. Neal laughed, too, shook his head at her. At them, it seemed.

"After that last time on the phone, when you said you were seeing her, I started thinking that you'd always looked at Kate with a certain something. I shouldn't have been surprised when you ended up together."

"Whatever you saw, it wasn't what you thought."

"Facts are facts," she said.

"I was probably seeing a flash of you in her."

"Stop saying that."

"Facts are facts," he said.

"We are nothing alike. *Nothing*."

"You are. You were."

"You just told me how she was so convincing that you left your children behind at her request. And I couldn't even convince you to come with me out west when you had nothing to lose but me if you stayed."

Neal dropped his head, gave a single nod. "That was a mistake."

"I don't want to get into it," Elin said.

"One would think that you taking off the way you did would have put out the fire. That, plus all the years, and everything that filled those years in between. But Kate knew. She knew me better than anyone. Even you."

Elin looked at him. "Don't."

"You'd think it would have been extinguished. Had enough bitterness thrown over it to dry the whole thing out."

"I need to get inside," Elin said.

"Well. It did, for a time. Simmered it, I guess. But all it takes is one swift fan of seeing you on the porch and up it goes again, proving her right."

Whatever fates they were tempting caught in her throat.

"You were cruel to stay with her," she said.

"I was."

"Even crueler to *have kids* with her."

"I can't argue with that."

"Stop being so agreeable."

"What do you want me to do?"

"Tell me the truth."

"I *am*. That's all I'm trying to do. There were three people in my marriage. Living a lie so huge was ruining both of us. The suffering in that house was unbearable. I started drinking. I *never* drank—surely you knew that about me. Other than a few beers here and there, I never did, and then one day a bloody mary at some firefighter brunch and I started asking myself why I didn't do that more often. Then I started doing it more often, which should have been a clue as to why it wasn't a great idea in the first place, but the thing is, it *was* a great idea. The days started to feel a little easier for me in equal proportion to that much harder for her."

"Jesus."

"Obviously, you can't raise two kids like that. You can't keep a job, or a wife you don't love, *especially* not when you're in love with her sister instead."

Elin's heel bounced beneath the bench. She chewed the side of a cuticle, caught herself, and stopped.

"I was a disaster, Elin. A first-class wrecking ball of a husband, father, and human being. When Kate lined up all my failures they were like tin soldiers on a coffee table, a whole army's worth staring me down. I did not stand a chance against my little flimsy self. I could not deny just how bad it was. And how perfect she appeared in the face of it. I asked her to forgive me, but then, how could she? Knowing that I wished the kids were ours, yours and mine—"

"Oh, God." Elin covered her eyes. "Stop. Please."

"And that doesn't even bring into account Averlee looking just like you. Your face in our house every damn day. Every day Kate saw me looking, remembering, wishing things were different, and yet, it was unbelievable how she loved that child, regardless."

Elin's eyes burned. She swallowed, released a long breath.

"What could I do? You understand? I loved those girls more than anything. I was willing to give up being their father if it meant they would have a better life. I was *convinced* that if I stayed I would ruin us all. So I moved out when she asked me to but that wasn't enough. Within weeks she came to my pathetic little apartment and begged me not to see them anymore. She said hearing about their visits with me was too hard on her. And she was beside herself when she said it, her face filled with such heartache, such devastation, which I know now may have had little, if anything, to do with me, and everything to do with her diagnosis, but in that moment I believed her, Elin. I cared about her, no matter how it might have seemed, then, or now, and I didn't want to hurt her, not anymore, not ever again. It wasn't hard to convince me. I'd nearly lost my job more than once. If it hadn't been for the guys at the firehouse covering for me I would have. I hated myself enough to buy into what she was saying. I believed that not everyone should be a parent. Certainly not me."

She couldn't fault him that, as much as she would like to, no, she could not fault him that.

"So I left."

"I hated you, too," Elin said. "Especially when I heard you'd gone."

"I didn't think so highly of you. Love, hate. It's a thin line."

"What did she tell you about me when I left? What did she say to lure you in?"

"Nothing. What do you mean?"

"What did she tell you that made it so easy for you to be with her?"

"She never said anything, not a bad word about you. It wasn't about that."

"Oh, please. I know you're lying, Neal. There's no way—"

"I was using her. That's what I was trying to explain."

"That's not the whole story. Not about my sister."

"You have no idea how busted up I was. If I could take it all back now I would. But then there's Averlee and Quincy—"

Elin stood. "I think I've heard enough."

"It was all me, Elin. I swear. *I* was the one who convinced *her*. Not the other way around."

Elin sat back down and held her head in her hands, fury building beneath her skin. How could she have been so wrong about so many people?

"If I hadn't ever called her the morning after you left, who knows how things might have turned out," Neal said.

"Yeah, well, lucky for us all you can't turn back time."

"Of course not."

"I mean it. You can't get back what you lost. Don't look at me that way. Leave it alone, Neal. Kate's gone. The girls are here. *That's it.*" She tossed her hands in the air. "That's all we have. End of story."

FORTY

THE FOLLOWING MORNING LILLIPUTIAN HANDS jostled Elin awake, and, like Gulliver, she felt large and heavy in the face of two tiny heads near her nose. She sprang up, assuming the worst. "Are you all right? What time is it?"

"Time for breakfast," Averlee said.

"Wow. How did I sleep in?" Elin began gathering her clothes from the chair.

"You don't have to hurry. We're going down now. With Daddy."

Elin froze, squeezing her shorts inside her fist. "I didn't realize you'd arranged that." Averlee was dressed in the red T-shirt and dark denim Elin had picked out for her. "That's fine," Elin said. "I'll be down in a bit."

"Come boy," Quincy said, and Fluke followed them out of the room.

By the time Elin had dressed, washed her face, and pulled her hair back, Neal and the girls had already eaten and were in the living room laughing at Fluke scratching his back on the rug. Elin passed through on the way into the dining room, offering a slight nod to Neal. Shug was in good spirits again, the whole house light and airy except for Elin. She was an intruder now. They had shut her out the minute he arrived. Even Shug had forgotten Elin, so taken by this man, by the reunion itself, by the picture of a family reunited, a long lost father returned.

Elin took two small bites of oatmeal already gone cold from her staring too long at the dusty books on the shelves. The coffee churned her stomach just as coldly. My sister didn't want this, she thought. Had Kate been buried she would surely be turning over in her grave.

A shared dinner alone so they could talk about Averlee and Quincy—this was all Neal wanted, all he said, giving nothing else away, except, "I need your advice," which gave her the urge to laugh until a sobering thought quickly brought her around: Whatever needed to be said, whatever was going to be decided, should not occur anywhere near the girls.

Now the evening had arrived so quickly. She slipped into her sheer, sleeveless dress, its slender hem resting just above her knees. She slid on her black leather sandals with a single strap across the top of her tanned foot and breathed in the smell of leather. Shug had agreed to watch the girls.

Elin insisted she and Neal drive separately, and she rounded the sidewalk to the Cuban diner, anticipating his face, his words, his *pleas* perhaps. Her leather purse on her shoulder thumped her ribs like a reminder, a poke in the side like a warning to watch herself. She'd pulled her hair into a twist at the back of her neck, and several strands had come loose near her eyes and several more in the form of small curls at the back of her neck, and she let them slide in the breeze, giving the impression of someone less complicated, some-one less wound up.

Year-round Christmas lights sparkled in the doorway, and blue and yellow curtains gave the evening sun a gauzy light. Neal was al-ready inside, waiting at a booth, the tips of his wispy hair a bit more under control as if still damp from a shower. His skin appeared tanner against his pale green shirt. Milky white buttons trailed down his chest, causing his teeth to flash even whiter when he smiled.

Mambo music streamed through the speakers, happy rhythms— trumpets, bongos, cowbells, and maracas. It filled the air with such immediacy that when Neal jumped up to greet her it was as if he'd been called to dance.

He thrust his hands into the pockets of his dark jeans. His smile was too eager for comfort, his skin lined by time and sorrow and clearly too much sun, all of which had somehow made him more appealing. Not more attractive, but rather had left a deeper character on his face.

"Elin," he said, and stepped toward her with his hands out as if to hug her. But then he seemed to think better of it, and turned instead to the booth. He waited for her to sit. A trace of the same lemony aftershave passed as he lowered himself onto the airy vinyl seat.

Elin picked up her fork, and laid it back down.

A man was suddenly placing menus on their table. "Nice to see you this evening." He bowed toward them both. "Let me know when you're ready."

Neal smiled at his back as he walked away.

"I'm sorry," Elin said quickly, before losing her nerve. "I wasn't very good at listening to you earlier."

"There's no need—"

"I apologize anyway."

The music shifted to a call and response, a chorus repeating the vocals, jazz horns mixed in between with bongos, the clicking of claves, and Elin felt a shift in the whole mood of the place, a shift within herself.

"So, I assume you quit drinking out there, in Arizona?"

Neal nodded with a faint smile as if the memories were spinning rapidly through his brain. He rubbed the back of his hand. "I'm no longer a firefighter."

"Oh."

"I work at a clinic now."

"A *clinic*? Doing what?"

"I'm a physician's assistant."

"Seriously?"

"Don't sound so surprised."

"But isn't that like a doctor or something? Didn't you have to go to school?"

"Yes. And yes. I did. I've been busy. I got busy and it saved my life."

"Do you like it?" She was having trouble picturing him shedding all that heavy gear, leaving behind the smell of soot for a crisp white coat, for a tongue depressor clamping down on sick tongues.

"I do. A lot. The pay is a whole lot more than what I used to make, and without the risk of dying on the job."

"Well, that's . . . great. Congratulations."

"I can't get over how much Averlee looks like you."

Elin glanced at the table.

"I'm sorry," he said.

"No. It's fine."

"It's hard not to say it. It's just so strange, seeing the two of you walk into a room, like—"

"What? Like what?" She could hear the agitation in her own voice.

"You seem really uncomfortable," he said. "We can go somewhere else where it might be easier to talk. Take a walk around the lake."

"What did you mean by 'seeing us walk into a room like,' what?"

"Nothing."

"Are you saying that when people see us together they'll just assume she's my daughter? That it all worked out in the end?"

"Elin. No. Come on."

The waiter returned. "Ready?" he asked.

"Sure," Neal said. "How about two of the specials on the board." He looked to Elin for approval. She clenched her jaw and nodded, reluctantly, and Neal handed the menus to the waiter, who glanced nervously at them both before turning away.

"I love Arizona," Neal said.

What was he getting at now? "I'm very fond of Oregon," Elin said.

"Never been."

"Never been to Arizona except for driving straight through to get here."

"It's nice."

"A lot of old people, I hear."

"A lot of rain in Oregon."

"Stop it, Neal," she said.

"It doesn't have to be so hard."

But it was, and she cast her eyes around the squares of white linoleum for fear of breaking under pressure if her attention were not quickly drawn elsewhere.

He slid his hand across the table though he didn't touch hers. Not quite. "How have the girls been since Kate died?"

"They're all right." She saw him looking at the pale circle on her finger where her wedding band used to be. He covered her whole hand with his own.

"I'm sorry about Kate. I know you two had your troubles, but"— he clasped her tighter—"I cared about her," he said, and Elin could see that this was true. "It's why I stayed, and it's why I left. Faulty as it was."

Elin concentrated on their joined hands, the sun streaming onto the checkered tablecloth that smelled of starch. She wondered if their memories differed, if they'd chosen to keep the same ones.

Hers that glint of recognition in his face when she came home after only hours away, the instantaneous rejoining of souls hoisted up in greeting. She remembered, in vivid detail, making love with him, scenes that returned over the years while straddling Rudi. Neal had a way of falling back onto his pillow and laughing afterward. At the wonder of it, she guessed. He had made her laugh, too.

Neal smiled, sadly, having no idea what was going through her mind, seeing only what must have been a faraway look, and he let go of her hand, leaned back, took a drink of water, and finally met her eyes.

"I don't think I can eat much right now," Elin said, thinking of how years ago she had left him right at the height of some power, sirens going off inside her head, on her way to save the day, tending to something larger than herself. And then she wasn't.

"I don't have much of an appetite either," he said.

"Kate wanted the girls to live with me," Elin said. "It's written in her will."

He stood and then scooted in next to her, his hip, his thigh against hers. He placed his arm on top of the seat behind her, the white buttons of his cuff resting coolly against the warm skin of her neck, and she could see the fine demarcation drawn at her feet, the division between one kind of happiness and another. She thought of her sister, of a line from an old song about how "love was not a victory march." One kind of happiness and another. She tried to prevent herself from seeing it, but couldn't.

FORTY-ONE

WINK HAD SLEPT ON VIVVIE'S sofa. She'd heard his restlessness through the night, the creak of the frame beneath his shifting weight. More than once she threw the blanket off her legs with the intention of going in there and telling him to go home to his own bed. But she couldn't bring herself to rise. Come morning she listened as he moved through her house, understanding that he did not want to leave her alone, not even for a minute, and she could feel him at intervals, standing in the doorway, looking down on her while she pretended to be asleep. She'd finally called out, "Good morning," and he brought her coffee with toast. She managed to take in half of each.

He sat with her now on the bed. Ten o'clock in the morning and she was still in bed. It hurt to open her eyes. "Do you think I need a doctor?" she asked.

"Do you feel like you need a doctor?"

"I just feel sick is all."

"You were pretty upset yesterday. Crying that hard will give you a hangover."

Vivvie caught his eyes, a slipstream of understanding, visions of him hidden away next door, grieving before she knew him.

"I want to see my daughter," she said.

"Which one?"

Vivvie smiled. "*Elin.*"

"Whew."

"You're a good man," she said, and he turned away as if embarrassed, patting her arm as he stood. Vivvie reached for his hand, big and warm and familiar to her now.

"You think maybe you could get Elin on the phone? Tell her it isn't about the girls. She doesn't need to bring them with her. She shouldn't bring them. She should come alone."

"I can do that."

"And would you mind bringing me the notebooks and letters? I think Elin should see them, too."

"Holy crap, Mom." Her mother was sitting in bed, face drawn, pink puffs rimming her bloodshot eyes. She appeared ancient, feeble compared to the robust woman Elin had seen just a week before. Kate's notebooks were piled atop the tangled blankets around her mother's legs. A stack of letters leaned against her knee and spilled onto her lap. Elin looked closely, recognizing Neal's handwriting.

"I'll be next door if you need anything," Wink said. Elin had forgotten he was there. He slipped down the hall and out the front door.

"What's going on?" Elin asked.

"Pull up the chair," her mother said.

"You look awful. How long have you been like this?" Elin asked.

"I need to talk to you."

"Are you sick?"

"I'm better than I was. Get the chair."

Elin dragged the kitchen chair with the broken cross stick to the bed, unease spreading quickly, her legs going soft, cheeks heating along the bone like a child with a fever, her mind loose and otherworldly. What was happening here? Something awful was happening here.

Elin sat, waited for her mother to speak, to stop picking at the hem of the sheet and address the spinning spheres of stories already soaring off the pages on the bed. She waited for her mother to wrap her arms around her skinny shoulders, to ward off the horrors, the wicked tales too chilling to be true.

"I know you know what happened that day in the woods," her mother said. "I know that Kate knew, too."

Elin shot to her feet. What to do? Duck? Run? Turn and fight? It was impossible to find a clear thought with an icy stream for veins. Her brain paralyzed, her arms and legs disabled. It was all she could do to make a slight turn so that her mother could not see her face.

"When you were a teenager, I said something to you that I regret, about the dog. You were asking about the blood on his head. You had every right. But I was scared. You had nothing but hate for me then, and even if you hadn't . . . Either way, I didn't know what else to say. So I lied."

Elin didn't move, didn't breathe as far as she could tell.

"I don't want to talk about the rest, about what happened out there with your father," her mother said. "I don't want to have to ex- plain myself. That's not what this is. I just want you to know how sorry I am for all the pain I caused you and Kate. It wasn't my inten- tion. You might find it hard to believe but I'd meant for the exact opposite, the absolute reverse of what took place."

She was crying now. Her mother was crying. When had Elin last heard her tears? Had she ever heard such a sound? Once. Beneath the window.

"I thought we could escape the grief. I wanted to spare you—"

"Mom. Don't."

"I want you to have Kate's notebooks."

"Fine."

"There are some beautiful poems in there."

"Whatever."

"Look at me."

Elin couldn't turn around. She knew if she did the day in the woods would appear in her mother's face, what her mother had done, the whole of what she'd *actually done* right there in her motherly eyes and mouth, because it *was* still there, of course it was, running fresh through her mother's mind all the time because how could it not? Her mother had a slaughter stuck inside her head, a stain clouding everything she ever looked at, or ever tried to see. Including Elin. Maybe especially Elin.

Elin punched the wall with the side of her fist.

"Don't," her mother said. "Please. Sit down."

Elin pounded again. "Fuck. Fuck. Fuck."

"Honey."

Honey? Elin thawed. She turned to face her mother. "I've always known. I just didn't want it to be true. I was and *still am* that little girl knowing, right here, right now, as if no time at all has passed, and I have no idea what to do with the weight of such a thing. What you're saying now doesn't make a difference to me. I wish I could say it did. That I think I understand now, as an adult, after seeing what Kate went through, that I understand at least *why* you did it, and that knowing is enough for me to say, 'Oh, all right, sure, mercy killing,' and all that. But you know what? It isn't true. I don't know if it can *ever* be true. It's suffocating." Elin held a fist to her chest.

"I'm not asking for forgiveness." Her mother clutched her hands together in her lap, lifted and let them fall softly, repeatedly.

"It *matters*, Mom. It just *does*. It so *completely* fucking *matters*."

"Please don't talk to me like that."

Elin burst out laughing. "*Don't talk to you like that?* We're past manners, don't you think?"

"No. I don't. And I'm not trying to make excuses—"

"I get that. There's nothing simple about any of this, no matter how many years I've spent trying to act like it never happened. Trying to pare it down into something digestible, something to look past, or barrel straight through. I couldn't, I can't—"

"I never meant for that to happen. You shouldn't have to—"

"I even used it against my own sister."

"What are you talking about?"

"I didn't comprehend the meaning of it. The *burden* of it. I was just a kid and it was like some urban legend or something, some scary story to frighten other kids, to frighten Kate. It wasn't real. It was, but it wasn't just the same."

"I never meant to hurt you and Kate."

"Do you regret it? What you did? Is that what you're saying?"

Her mother hesitated, eyes widening, mouth open, working up the words that would not come.

"Jesus, Mom!" Elin shook her head at the ceiling, trying to temper the tangle of emotion in her gut.

"I don't expect you to understand," her mother said. "I'm not *asking* you to understand."

"How can you not wish to take it back?"

"Because I loved him more than I hated the act of what I did."

"Really. *Really?* You weren't *just* his wife, you know. You were our *mother,* too."

"I'm sorry you ever learned the truth of it."

Elin plopped into the chair, defeated. "Don't you get it? The point is, *you* were shaped by it, Mom. It changed *you.* And my knowing the truth, well, I guess my *facing* the truth, actually helps in the end. It helps to explain why you were such an awful mother."

Elin met her mother's flinty stare.

"I'm sorry," Elin said, "but mothering was not your forte." It sounded like something Averlee would say, the smart tone of it. A small laugh crept into the corner of Elin's mouth.

Her mother's, too.

Elin shook her head at the floor, drew her elbows in, and leaned forward as if speaking to her shoes. "Seeing the dog like that, and then the way you treated us with such distance, I mean we had lost our father. We lost him and then we lost you. It did a number on me, not to mention Kate. I'm not trying to fill you with any more guilt. I'm sure you've got plenty to keep you company. But you need to understand that I'm sitting here holding onto every bit of grace I own, which isn't a lot, I'll grant you that, but what I have does not help me see past what you did."

Her mother leaned forward, touched her knee. "I'm not asking anything of you at all. I'm sorry. That's all. I wanted to say I'm sorry and you don't have to say or do anything. You don't have to accept it or reject it. I just didn't want to die and you never know."

Elin looked her straight in the face. She seemed to be aging right before her eyes. They would never speak of this again, and that was fine. That was what she wanted. "I'm done here," Elin said.

"What do you mean?"

"This is my Chief Joseph moment. I will fight no more forever."

"There is no one to fight, Elin. Nothing left to fight about."

"The girls are going home with Neal."

Her mother swallowed.

"He'll let you visit them anytime you want," Elin said. "He'll bring them here to see you, he will. And you can go out there. Stay for weeks at a time. He said so."

"But Kate wanted them to be with you. She wanted you to raise them."

"I know, Mom, and I can't say I'm not moved by the gesture. But it wasn't as simple or straightforward as that. Her intention didn't stop there. I see what she was trying to do. By giving me guardianship she meant to pull me into the mix. She knew the law would give them to Neal. Of course she did. But in the midst of trying to sort it all out, Neal and I would have been forced together again. I guess she thought that was all it would take for us to live happily ever after."

Vivvie reached for one of the letters, unfolded the page. "I never liked the idiot for obvious reasons, you know that, but there's no denying why you and Kate both had a thing for him. That soft-soap voice, that hair. He was always polite. I'll give him that. But listen here. These are the letters he wrote to Averlee and Quincy. Kate never even opened them. Curiosity would have gotten the best of me. But not Kate. She just filed them away, saving them for some other purpose. Here he is telling Averlee and Quincy what it's like out there where he lives. 'Mountains red as fire. Cactus wrens like lovebirds, coming round in pairs . . .'"

"Quite the poet himself," Elin said.

"Either that or a con artist, putting on airs."

"Somehow I just don't see that."

"Me neither. I've just disliked him for so long it's hard to change course."

"I know how that is." Elin blew the air from her chest with a burst. "I've got a lot of things to figure out. I need to go back to my life. Not to Rudi, but back to the life I was trying to get to in the first place. I'm sorry. But I guess you already knew that there was no way I was going to stay here. Not that you asked me to. Not that you want me to."

Her mother smiled sadly. "The minute I saw you in my kitchen, when I said it looked like life was treating you well out there, I could see it wasn't all true. I could see the trouble in you, but I saw the traces of something lighter, too, something you gained from leaving here. I don't blame you for going. You deserve to be happy, Elin. Go on. You've got nothing to be sorry for."

"I've got plenty to be sorry for."

"Well, I'm afraid I've got you beat there."

Elin gave a snort for a laugh. "Yeah. You're the winner, all right. Or the loser."

Her mother winced.

"Sorry."

"It's all right." She smirked and shook her head. "How does that old song go? 'Gloom, despair, and agony on me'?"

"'Deep dark depression, excessive misery.'"

"That's it," her mother said. "Story of my life."

"You're laughing, though. I don't remember you ever being much for laughter. Must be that neighbor of yours getting under your skin."

"He's just the lawn boy."

"I'll bet he is."

Her mother smiled, looked toward the window as if embarrassed. The window faced Wink's house. "When do you plan on leaving?"

"Today."

"Oh." Vivvie pushed herself to the side of the bed with her fists and let her legs hang over the bed. "I'll come visit this time, if you still want me to," she said. "I'm not returning to Roth's. I decided to retire. Time is on my side now," she said.

Elin leaned forward and wrapped her arms around her mother. "Of course you can come visit. You can bring the girls with you, too. The fancy life, Mom," she whispered, and they both gave a small laugh. "You and that lawn boy ought to take a cruise."

FORTY-TWO

ELIN HAD TRIED TO IMAGINE their wild hair flapping in misty ocean breezes, the three of them together, crouched near a lighthouse in search of anemones in tide pools. She tried with deep conviction to picture herself helping with homework, with doing their hair, and making waffles on the weekends. She imagined driving through the Willamette Valley of tulips, mint, and vineyards. Imagined they were on their way to the mountain. "What's all that?" the girls would ask. "Hops and grapes for beer and wine," she'd say, and then their eyes, their gasps, their joy on the mountaintop beneath the falling snow.

But after weeks of trying to visualize this shared life together, a palpable impression never would form. What she clearly saw was her nieces slipping in and out of her life—holiday visits, emails, birthday and graduation cards filled with cash. What she saw was herself in the role of an aunt.

Now here she was saying good-bye to Shug in the kitchen. Good-bye to everything that might have been, all that could have begun in the rooms of this house but had instead come to an end. Elin thanked and hugged Shug for longer than a person comfortably ought to after having known her for such a short time, but Shug held tight and stroked Elin's hair the way a mother would stroke a child's.

"Well, come on now, darlin'," Shug said. "You act like you're saying some farewell finale here. Send me a line when you get a chance. I'd love to hear from you."

"Of course you'll hear from me. And you know where to find me, too. It's not all rain. Come see for yourself." Elin squeezed her again, sure she'd still be thinking of Shug years from now, and this house, and the way Shug had helped Elin take care of Averlee and Quincy, the way she'd looked after Fluke, but mostly the lesson she taught Elin about breezy contentment, an example of compassion, of how to live alone.

But for now the stairs felt like a death march. Averlee and Quincy were waiting for her in the room they'd shared, waiting for their lives to split apart.

They had piled into an armchair with Fluke, all three staring out the window at Elin's packed car in the driveway. Elin kneeled beside them and Quincy wriggled free of the chair and grabbed onto her neck, held it as if she had no intention of letting go. She kissed Elin's cheek, a small warm pucker of electricity. Elin had never loved a child before, and now she loved two. It was a terrible heartbreak kind of love, a severing and reassembling in a slightly altered order.

When Quincy lessened her hold Elin pulled a small box of postcards from her purse. Old Florida scenes of fruit crates, gators, and Weeki Wachee mermaids. "You can practice your writing on me. Tell me anything. Everything. What it's like in Arizona. Keep me up on the latest with your sister."

Averlee had been watching the two of them, but at the mention of her name she turned her face to the window, petting Fluke in long strokes down his back.

"Thank you," Quincy said. Several hugs later she was off down the hall with Fluke, playing and petting and laughing, though softly, and Elin wondered if she was making a conscious effort to respect the somber mood they were caught in, or if her careful quiet just came naturally, an innate understanding of how things worked without having to think.

Elin stood. "Are most of your things gathered in there?" she asked, gesturing toward the suitcase on the floor. "You still have some time. You aren't leaving until tomorrow."

"Then why are you leaving today?"

What could she say? Her own cowardliness had her on the run? That having to watch them drive off and leave her there alone was more than she thought she could bear? That she was afraid it might make her change her mind? "I've got a long way to go," Elin said. "Even if I leave today I won't get there for four or five days. You'll be in Arizona in just a few hours on a plane."

Averlee was quiet.

"So your things are in the suitcase, then?"

"Mostly," Averlee said. "Yeah."

"Thanks for helping your sister."

Averlee didn't look at her.

"It's going to be fine. You two are in good hands."

Averlee scratched the back of her hand, her sights still on the window.

"Come here," Elin said, her arms open, and Averlee came forward, her face partially tucked into her neck, shoulders drawn as if to hide the grief building in her face, tears twisting her against her will.

Elin's arms wrapped around her niece in a desperate grip that nearly frightened her. She hadn't quite seen it coming, not like that, and hoped she hadn't hurt the small bones entrusted to her. She did not want to fall apart in front of Averlee, told herself over and over not to, but then wondered if maybe she should. If maybe she was *supposed* to. Was staying strong the thing? Or openly expressing her sorrow? She'd have to be a monster to let a child cry against her like that and not show some emotion. She wasn't a monster. Clearly. While her mind was busy analyzing dumb ideas, her own tears had made a run for it.

"You'll come visit," she said through the snot that was now running, too. "Spend whole summers with me, if you like."

Averlee sobbed and Elin understood what Averlee could not say, perhaps not even inside her own head. Elin couldn't love Neal the way Neal loved her. She could never be an ideal part of their lives. She would not be stepping in as a mother figure, helping in that way to mend the ruptured life her sister had left behind. Her role would always be that of aunt. Elin hoped Averlee understood, if not now then please someday, she thought, giving her an extra squeeze, someday she said to herself like a prayer, let this girl and her sister, but especially this one here, let her know that Elin could not lift her away from the injustice of it all, no matter how badly she wanted, she couldn't keep Averlee from having to absorb the world's achy, lopsided weight. The power was not all hers.

"You're lucky to have a daddy," Elin said into the top of Averlee's head. "I never had one. Not that I remember well enough. Your mother didn't either."

"Yes she did. He looked just like her."

Elin held her out, wiped her face.

"How do you know that?"

"I saw a picture."

"Where?"

"At Grandma's."

"Really?"

"It's in a box."

"What box?"

Averlee shrugged.

"Are you sure?"

Averlee held onto her again, nodding into her chest.

"Well. I'll have to ask Grandma about it. I've never seen it." Elin rocked her gently in the quiet. "Can you tell me something before I go? About what your mother said, about me keeping secrets?"

Averlee's shoulders stiffened.

"Why did she tell you that?"

"She didn't want Quincy and me to be like you."

Elin laughed. "Ha. Well. Mission accomplished. You're nothing like us."

"That's not true."

"Isn't it?"

"We're like our mom."

"Oh. Of course you are. You're a lot like your mom. You both are. Of course."

"She said she had some secrets, too."

"Ah. Well. I guess she did."

"You sound just like her. You remind me of her."

"I'll take that as a compliment."

"She wouldn't tell me the secrets, though." Averlee said.

"They aren't secrets once you tell."

"That's exactly what she said."

"Some things are better left unsaid."

"She said that, too."

FORTY-THREE

NEAL HAD PACKED THE CAR the night before, and now the sun was barely on the rise as he wrangled his daughters into the backseat like little drunks, crawling, fumbling, squinting beneath the harsh overhead light. He slid up front and reached over the seat to help settle them in, but Averlee had already buckled Quincy's seat belt, handed her the white fleece blanket from Shug, and tucked her own, in blue, between her shoulder and the door. Both girls stared straight ahead, hands folded on laps, expressionless eyes, waiting for the next thing.

Neal hit the automatic lock button and all four doors bolted, shutting off the interior light, and the quiet of the car, the smell of new upholstery, expanded in the dark.

Having them now did not mean the years of grief would stand down and leave him alone. He guessed the opposite was closer to the truth. Having them brought it all back. Even when he wasn't thinking about the past, he was forced to think about the future, forced to grieve all that would never be. Elin was never going to walk through the door and take him back. Kate was never going to forgive him. He would have to learn how to give all that up, hand it in once and for all, in exchange for all that suddenly was.

"All set back there?" he asked, facing forward now, holding tight to the steering wheel. Elin had surprised him with a knock on his door before she left, and then surprised him again when she let him kiss her good-bye, when she kissed him back, long and hard, an ever-lasting kiss that went beyond two people parting in a doorway.

Averlee gave a thumbs-up in the mirror. Neal fastened his own belt, took one final look at the house, the dark windows, the empty bench on the porch. The pink and yellow sunrise was vanishing the stars on the horizon, others still clinging in the black through the sky-light above their heads.

"Tell us again what it looks like," Averlee said as soon as Neal backed out of the driveway.

"Well. Let's see. The mountains are red as fire," he said. "And a creek in the backyard is shallow enough for you to wade in, with soft round rocks, and the deer like to stop by in the early mornings and evenings for a drink."

"And there are spiny lizards," Quincy said.

"How do you know?" Averlee asked.

"I told her about them. Funny toads and spiny lizards and cactus like the ones you see in cartoons."

They were quiet for so long Neal thought they might have fallen asleep. Then Averlee smiled at him in the mirror.

"I remember you from before," she said.

"You do?"

"I remember the lake you took me to. We were in a giant swan boat."

"That's *right*. You remember that? I'm surprised. You were so young."

"And a real bird landed on the boat."

"*Yes*," he said. "It did. You're right. A pelican. And it scared you."

"*Scared* me. Why?"

"They're huge, with giant feet and long beaks. A wingspan bigger than you are now."

"I don't remember being scared."

"That's good," he said, and watched as Averlee sunk against the window, eyes gazing in the direction of the pines. "I'm glad to hear it." Quincy rested her cheek on Averlee's shoulder and closed her eyes. What Neal didn't say was that even as he'd chased the pelican off, even as he told her there was nothing to be afraid of, pulled her against him, covered her small body with his arm, told her he was right there, *I'm right here*, even as this was happening, he was already planning on leaving her, already packed to go away.

Averlee's lids bobbed, closed for a moment, and shot back open. It was clear she was fighting sleep. "It's all right, Ave," Neal said. "Get some rest. I'll wake you at the airport."

She glanced at her sleeping sister on her shoulder, yawned, and cleared her throat. "I'm not tired," she said. "The early bird gets the worm."

"You are, too," Quincy said without opening her eyes.

Within seconds Averlee had sunk against the door, mouth open, her head lost in what must have been a deep state of dreams, waking only when Neal jostled her arm, took her hand, and led her, gently, from the car.

PART FOUR

FORTY-FOUR

THE FOLLOWING YEAR WINK STOOD in front of Vivvie's bathroom sink across the hall from where she lay in bed, watching him through the open bedroom door. He was wearing a white T-shirt and white boxers that drooped in the seat. He shaved in slow, deliberate lines, his free hand cupped beneath the razor, careful not to drip any foam on the sink. When he finished he tapped the razor twice below the faucet, and flushed away flecks of whiskers left behind. He dried his face with a towel down the same lines he had shaved, smiled at himself in the mirror, and smacked his cheeks.

He came in and flopped next to her, smelling of aftershave and toothpaste.

"It's Quincy's birthday, week after next," she said.

"Lucky seven," he said.

Vivvie nodded, thinking of Averlee and Quincy's pictures all over the fridge, the way each girl had begun to resemble Kate around the mouth and in the shape of their eyes, especially when they smiled. Vivvie missed Kate. All those years she was gone were nothing compared to the year that just passed. Hope of ever seeing her again had vanished into smoke, literally, the day her daughter was cremated. Vivvie was still learning how to let go of what she could, how to live with all the rest.

"I've had her birthday marked on the calendar every year for the past six years," she said. "This is the first one that I'll actually get to talk to her."

On their backs, they stared at the ceiling.

"Seven years old," Vivvie said. "Don't seem possible."

"Don't seem possible I've nearly lived as long as the average American male," Wink said. "Nearly reached my expiration date, and I don't feel a day over thirty, least not in my head. Maybe closer to fifty in the lower back."

Vivvie studied the thin lines around his mouth and eyes, decades of frowns and sorrows, of laughter and too much sunshine—his whole life story written on his face. "I know what you mean," Vivvie said. "I feel younger than I did twenty years ago."

Wink smiled, lingering on her longer than usual.

"Thank you," she said.

He lifted her hand and kissed the top of it. "You ought to try and see her on her birthday."

"You mean fly out there?"

"Why not?"

"You want to go?"

"Why not?"

"We've never been on a plane together," she said, and pictured them on a flight, eating peanuts, watching a movie, nothing remarkable, feeling extraordinary.

"I need to ask you something," Wink said. "I've got something I need to ask. I was going to wait a bit, but now, I don't know, your mention of flying off together. I think it's important to be spontaneous in this life. To act when the moment calls for it, and so, well . . ."

He kneeled on the floor, winced, and lifted his knees back up, one by one, squatting now, only his head and shoulders visible above the edge of the bed. Then he held up a small box and sat next to Vivvie.

He was still in his underwear, taking her hand in his. He cleared the way in his throat for a string of seriousness. She could see what was coming. Clear as a train about to run her down in the dark, she could see it, and wondered if she forgot how to talk, how to breathe.

The following week she stopped by the College Park strip mall to look at the ready-mades in the Mr. Right Bridal Gowns and More store. The sweet, early morning scent of honeysuckle floated above the cool, nighttime asphalt as she studied the shapely mannequins in the window display; their big blond wigs, black eyeliner, and peach colored lips reminded her of the brides of yesteryear. They reminded her of the first time she married.

"Mrs. Fenton? Is that you?"

Vivvie tightened the purse strap across her shoulder and turned. A man dressed in a white IZOD shirt and khaki Dockers approached her in the parking lot.

"It's Officer Moore. I was on duty when you came to pick up your granddaughters that night."

Vivvie took a step back, made a visor with her hand, and stiffened with fear unfolding. Was this it? Had they turned her in after all? Made it seem as if she were free and clear while they gathered their case against her? Happy for the first time in decades. That's what she thought, happy for the first time in decades, again and again the same thought. She nearly spoke the words out loud.

"Yes," Vivvie said. "I know who you are."

Visions of Wink and Elin conspiring during late night phone calls came to her now, arrived like a note on a platter, filled with a detailed explanation of their masterful trick, the real reasons behind the "kindness" they had shown her this past year.

"How's those granddaughters of yours?"

"Well. They're all right. They'll be all right, under the circumstances." Vivvie glanced at the mannequins. At least her granddaughters were so far away. They'd never even know what had happened to her. This was a blessing, she guessed. Something to be grateful for. "I guess you know my daughter is no longer with us. First my husband, and then my child."

"I'm sure sorry to hear that," Moore said.

She gazed back and forth between Moore and the brides. "I appreciate it." She shifted her weight, the delicate and poised young brides mocking her from behind the air-conditioned glass.

She braced for the words she'd been bracing against for more than thirty years: *Vivien Fenton, you are under arrest for the murder of your husband, Jackson Fenton.*

"Well?" Vivvie said. "What's it going to be?"

"Oh, you know. I just thought I'd say hello. People down at the station still talk about those granddaughters of yours. They just struck everybody. Something really special about them. Broke everybody's heart."

Vivvie nodded slowly. "Yes," she said. "Thank you. Thank you for telling me that."

She glanced again at the mannequins, but the thought of a wedding, the thought of *marriage*, caused her mouth to go dry and her feet to thicken against the insides of her open-toed shoes.

"Good luck, then," Moore said, and Vivvie said the same, considering the daily calamities that made up the hours of this man's life. It occurred to her that for some, trouble was fundamental, a way of life, essential, even, for them to be the person they aimed to be.

She drew in the smell of honeysuckle, and then the sound of fast traffic at the corner.

"Take care," Moore said.

"You, too," Vivvie said, raising her hand as they parted, feeling the brides of yesteryear at her back. She had been wrong about so many things. There wasn't enough time left in this world for making more mistakes. Wink had loved her for so long, yet never spoke a word of it, just sat with the feeling, and how strange to think that the love they had existed before she was even in it, while she was still wandering around blindly unaware.

She loved him. Loved him in her bed, in his bed, in both their kitchens and bathrooms. She loved their two lives overlapping, the way they met in the middle, sometimes literally for a picnic in the yard. She loved how she made breakfast at her place and he grilled dinner at his as if they lived on a campground, a couple of travelers having an adventure. Would it be the same if they confined themselves to one home or the other the way marriage would certainly call for?

They'd already gotten it right. The same way Kate had in her final years, knowing exactly what to do with the time that was left. Knowing how to make a life mean something, to wring out its worth when it was right there in one's hands instead of just wishing about it afterward, or imagining how it could have been, or should have been, different. There wouldn't be a wedding, Vivvie thought. This is how we do it right.

FORTY-FIVE

AVERLEE COULD HAVE SWORN SHE felt herself growing overnight, growing into "a leggy, galloping girl," her dad said, "a Great Dane tripping
over her own paws," which made her laugh. He measured her and
Quincy in pencil marks on the kitchen wall and she'd shot up an inch
in the last month alone. "All that running around outdoors," her dad
said. "Fresh air and dry heat. You're a eucalyptus, Ave, standing tall
in the sunshine, right where it loves to be."

Averlee would live outside if she could, collecting rocks and nam-
ing fish in the creek where she waded barefoot. The creek turned out
rocks like jewels, a magical stream with amethyst, azurite, and mala-
chite, broken loose from the mines upstream. For weeks there'd be
nothing and then there'd be a chip of turquoise trimmed in copper.
Once she found what looked like a yellow diamond, and her dad said
it was a rare piece of peridot. He bought her a book of gems so she
could match them to the pictures on the page. At night the hallway
light shined onto the shelf above Quincy's bed where Averlee kept
her treasures, and the last things she saw before heading into her
dreams were blues and greens and a shimmer of coppery gold.

But perhaps what she loved most about living there, besides having her dad, was the pair of cactus wrens in the saguaro out back.
Averlee owned a set of binoculars and wore them around her neck all
day the way other girls wore a necklace, and every morning began on
the back patio with her *spyglasses*, as Quincy called them, pinned to

her eyes as the wrens popped free their heads from their burrow. She knew their catalogue of calls by heart, the *tek, tek, tek* that reminded her of automatic sprinklers in Florida, and the croaky, scratchy song they made when the squirrels came too close. Her dad showed her how curious the birds were, that if she placed anything they hadn't seen before on the patio table, the wrens would come out to investigate. A pink Barbie shoe from Quincy's collection might be found next to a white plastic spoon and a stick of orange glue. Today, when they rolled Quincy's birthday bike into the garage, the wrens followed it through the back door and out the other side.

Now she watched as her dad taught her sister to ride her new birthday bike. It had taken more than half a year of her dad telling Averlee that she didn't have to do everything for Quincy, that all the worrying and cleaning up and keeping her sister on track was in fact *his* job. Her job was to be a kid. To find gems in the creek and look at birds and go to school and do her homework. That was it. She didn't know how it was possible to feel heavier and lighter at the same time but that was how she felt with her dad, with her mom gone, with the wrens poking their heads out of the cactus.

He gripped the back of Quincy's bike seat, and ran alongside her with promises that he would never in million years let her fall, and yet Quincy still shrieked that he better not let go. Quincy preferred the indoors, a corner by herself to read a book. "She was the still point from which Averlee spun around," whatever that meant, her dad had written in an email to Aunt Elin. When his work called he often took the phone into another room, accidentally forgetting what he'd left on the computer screen.

"Sometimes I catch Quincy looking up from the pages of her book, eyes fixed somewhere across the room, and I believe she's in heavy thought about her mother," her dad wrote. Her aunt Elin wrote back, "It must be hard having to walk a constant tightrope of understanding, trying to keep her from falling too far into herself, while keeping the memory of Kate alive."

After that it hurt too much and Averlee stopped peeking.

Her grandmother and Wink were flying in today by dinnertime. "You can show off to Grandma!" Averlee yelled down the street. She was losing patience with her sister, and maybe it came out in her voice, or maybe the thought of her grandmother seeing what Quincy could do was where Quincy found the courage, but whatever the reason the mystery of balance was suddenly hers.

Half an hour later Quincy still streamed up and down the street on her white bike in her white tennis shoes and white shorts like a ghost girl discovering new powers.

Averlee and her dad waited at the end of the driveway for Quincy to loop back around and they would clap every time, and after Quincy figured out how to wave with one hand on the handlebar, the other in the air, they clapped even harder, and around and around her sister went, and it never seemed to get old.

FORTY-SIX

LATE NOVEMBER. ELIN HAD SOLD the house she owned with Rudi last year. Her new house sat in a clearing on a small red cliff facing the Pacific Ocean. At the edge of her property an eastern wall of rocky earth dropped a hundred feet onto the shore. Modest cedar shingles and bright white trim made up her carriage house, surrounded by purple hydrangeas, yellow irises, domes of intensely sweet daphne near the doors. A chalky white lighthouse with a cardinal-red roof loomed to the north, the view from Elin's kitchen sink where she liked to wash dishes by hand. Beyond the long living room windows wind-swept Madronas stacked to the west, their orange-red bark curling in thin sheets, exposing the satiny green sheen underneath. At night the crash of the ocean, the rumble of its storms became the lullabies that eased Elin into sleep.

Her mother told her about the fire, and how that singular photograph had somehow survived, whether misplaced inside the house or carried back into the house inside a pocket or the folds of a chair. She didn't know. But she felt compelled to hold onto it, to save it like "a dog cheating euthanasia," she'd said, and then fell silent at the bad taste of her joke, but Elin had laughed anyway, which seemed a good sign, considering.

Elin had the original restored and sealed away, but an enlarged copy hung in a frame above her fireplace in the living room. Every morning she woke to her father swinging her sister through the air.

It was as much a memorial to them both as it was a reminder that loving someone, loving anyone, even those long gone, was of consequence, and not loving them was of consequence, too.

"Let's go, boy." Elin stepped from the house, holding tight to the urn with Kate's ashes, Fluke running circles around her feet. He dashed ahead as she closed the front door, and the air smelled of cherry firewood, pine, and sea salt. She followed him down the steep path through the sharp beach grass and onto the shore. She liked seeing it all change with fall, the juniper at her back already gone a burnt, reddish brown.

The black, canoe-sized logs scattered on the beach had changed their shape again, some by force of tides, others by young people dragging them into bonfires. During the summer months yellow blazes lit up the beach, and the ocean wind carried campfire songs all the way to Elin's front porch. The ballads of drunken teenagers, families lost in hopeless, scattered choirs, couples harmonizing love songs on guitar.

Ropey brown piles of tubular sea kelp were strewn everywhere today, the sky unusually cloudless. Elin plopped down near the dunes, gently screwed the pearl-white urn into the sand, and tossed a stick for Fluke. They were alone save the man on a paddleboard in the distance. It used to be only surfers but now paddleboarding was the thing of the day. The man appeared to know what he was doing. Not everyone did. His strokes were long and steady and he didn't fall off, not while she was watching. His body was framed in the baby-blue sky; the long white stripes on his wet suit reflected the sun. She'd seen him before. She thought she had. Always in the water.

He paddled away from her, and Elin thought of "sneaker waves," the way they appeared without warning, a tow with Mack-truck strength heaving bodies and boats out to sea. They were impossible to predict, like an earthquake—no warning, just coming when it came. But today the sun shined, and the air let go a weak, pleasant breeze, and Elin felt an opening in her chest. It wasn't happiness so much as being on the verge of happiness, perched up there, readying to flee. She did not know why the beast that had come for her sister and father had not come for her. It may yet, of course. There was a blood test she could take, but what was the point? It was either coming for her or it wasn't. No prevention. No cure. Her only concern was for her nieces. She wasn't one for praying but if there was any justice in the world, even the smallest bit of rhyme or reason, she implored it to wrap them up inside, to follow wherever they might be.

She'd read Neal's letters to them before her mother returned the stack. This was a man who deserved a greater love than Elin could have offered. That was the simple truth, and she was right to get out of the way. It was also true that she loved him more than she thought she did after reading what he wrote to his children. But not every kind of love called for action. Some demanded one stay put, allowing for nothing more than it to be exactly as it was.

He was happy. "Most days parenting feels a lot like running stop signs on desert back roads," he wrote in a recent email. "A no-hands hurtle through the great wide open, a thrill never without risk. You tried to teach me this years ago, how getting to the good stuff required a free fall into the unknown, that that was where the real joy would always be waiting. The prize was at the bottom, gambles and perils and hazards be damned."

Kate had understood this better than anyone, bravely walking away from the world she'd been given to enter one of her own creation. Elin read Kate's notebooks, and then stored them in a box in her basement. She had no intention of showing them to anyone, nor of mentioning what was written there, not even to Neal. She often thought of making a bonfire, and believed that one day soon she would set fire to her sister's words, let their smoke gust sideways out to sea where Kate was about to churn for all of eternity. Kate had asked for the quiet ritual of today, but she would appreciate the fiery spectacle of flaming notebooks, too. For now, Elin needed to have something of her sister's in the house, her words like a presence on days when Elin felt a little too mournful, a little too separated from all the people who had truly known her.

A bald eagle glided overhead toward the clump of pines on the hill. They were common out this way. All one had to do was look up. Hadn't her mother tried to take her and Kate to see one once? She didn't remember much about that, but the idea of it struck her with a vague appreciation.

It was all laid out before her now, the whole messy past, and she'd done everything in her power to put things right. No doubt she'd come up short, and that, she believed, was what it meant to be alive. The absence of answers and perfection allowed for the wonder, mistakes for tripping trap doors to the glimmering unforeseen. But she had come so far, too, gazing at the ocean and recalling her sister with fondness, with ease. Saving Kate from drowning meant Averlee and Quincy could one day exist, and Elin had given those same children to Neal by walking out on him, by cutting the tie so severely. That was one way to look at it.

But she felt great. That was the truth. No headaches in six months. She'd read that this could happen with age. People outgrew migraines. But she couldn't help thinking it had more to do with being at the ocean, this cape, the cool blue colors of her days mixed with charcoal and silvery driftwood, winter skies a white-ash swath as far as the eye could see.

Did humans have habitats? It was a question she'd asked Neal the other day in an email. "I feel so alive in my own skin out here," she wrote. He'd sent back a picture of Averlee with a huge grin while pan-

ning for gems in a creek, another of Quincy, her face a study in seren-
ity as she read beneath a lamp. "Yes," he wrote. "I believe they do."

The paddleboarder waved in her direction. Elin checked behind
her. There was no one she could see. The man shook his wet hair
from his face and neck and waved again. She waved back, fanning her
arm above her head, not minding if he'd mistaken her for someone
else. She stood, brushed the sand from her clothes, cradled the urn in
her arm, and headed toward the levee of boulders, an earthly path
jutting out into the riptide.

That same opening, that same verging happiness returned with
the feel of flesh and blood and heat. She thought of her father swinging her sister, her mother capturing the moment for all time. Elin had
captured it, too, understanding, even then, that the moment had
meant something, that the world could change in an instant, and she
needed to be mindful of where she was, to live with intention, to always recognize the deliberateness of love.

ACKNOWLEDGMENTS

I WOULD LIKE TO THANK Sharon Harrigan, Leigh Rourks, Pete Fromm, Bonnie Jo Campbell, Jack Driscoll, Vera Wildauer, Jacque Ben-Ze-kry, Terry Goodman, Andrew Bartlett, Charlotte Herscher, Melissa Crisp, and Andrew Reed. All of you played an important part in this work, and I am so grateful.

ABOUT THE AUTHOR

ANDREW REED, 2012

DEBORAH REED IS THE AUTHOR of the novel *Carry Yourself Back to Me*, a Best Book of 2011 Amazon Editors' Pick. She is also the author of the bestselling thriller *A Small Fortune* and its sequel, *Fortune's Deadly Descent*, written under the pen name Audrey Braun. All three novels have been translated or are forthcoming in German. Deborah holds a master of fine arts (MFA) degree in creative writing (fiction) and teaches at UCLA's Extension Writing Program, as well as at workshops and conferences around the United States and in Europe. She lives in Los Angeles, California.